The Final Folly of Captain Dancy
&
Other Tall Tales

OTHER BOOKS BY LAWRENCE WATT-EVANS

Vika's Avenger
The Chromosomal Code
Touched by the Gods
The Rebirth of Wonder
The Nightmare People
One-Eyed Jack
Among the Powers
Shining Steel
(with Esther M. Friesner) *Split Heirs*
(with Carl Parlagreco) *The Spartacus File*

THE ADVENTURES OF TOM DERRINGER
Tom Derringer and the Aluminum Airship
Tom Derringer in the Tunnels of Terror
Tom Derringer and the Steam-Powered Saurians
Tom Derringer and the Electrical Empire

THE CASES OF CARLISLE HSING
Nightside City
Realms of Light

THE FALL OF THE SORCERERS
A Young Man Without Magic
Above His Proper Station

THE ANNALS OF THE CHOSEN
The Wizard Lord
The Ninth Talisman
The Summer Palace

THE OBSIDIAN CHRONICLES
Dragon Weather
The Dragon Society
Dragon Venom

THE LORDS OF DÛS
The Lure of the Basilisk
The Seven Altars of Dûsarra
The Sword of Bheleu
The Book of Silence

LEGENDS OF ETHSHAR
The Misenchanted Sword
With A Single Spell
The Unwilling Warlord
Taking Flight
The Blood of a Dragon
The Spell of the Black Dagger
Night of Madness
Ithanalin's Restoration
The Spriggan Mirror
The Vondish Ambassador
The Unwelcome Warlock
The Sorcerer's Widow
Relics of War
Stone Unturned
Charming Sharra

The Final Folly of Captain Dancy

&

Other Tall Tales

Ten Stories from Other Histories

by

Lawrence Watt-Evans

Misenchanted Press

Bainbridge Island

The Final Folly of Captain Dancy

& Other Tall Tales

Cover design by Lawrence Watt-Evans

Published by Misenchanted Press
www.misenchantedpress.com

Contents

Introduction

There is a genre of fiction that does not, so far as I know, have a name. It's not historical fantasy, because the history isn't accurate enough to deserve that name; it borrows historical trappings, but mixes and matches them to create a never-was land of adventure unconfined by inconvenient facts.

Disney's Pirates of the Caribbean films are an example -- they happily mix and mangle three different centuries, playing fast and loose with geography as well as history. Several westerns also blur various decades of the 19th century, and ignore differences between, say, Texas and Kansas and California, treating them all as "the West."

Zorro's adventures take place in a California that doesn't happen to match any actual time. There are samurai movies that don't correspond to real history, and innumerable stories set in a China that never was. Stories of ancient Rome often fail to distinguish one century from the next.

Purists may complain that these stories mislead and confuse readers, but the truth is, it's much easier to just have fun with a story when you don't worry about whether the setting makes any sense.

In an earlier version of this book I called these "pseudo-historical fantasy," but I've decided that they're really just tall tales, not meant to be believed.

I don't write them very often; I prefer to invent settings from whole cloth and write straight fantasy, or actual science fiction. Sometimes, though, I indulge myself, and this is a collection of those stories.

"The Final Folly of Captain Dancy" is set in days of sail, among islands that include British outposts, but it makes no attempt to be historically accurate. I don't even know whether it's set in the Caribbean or the Pacific, or in the 18th century or the 19th; it doesn't matter. It's a fantasy.

"Windwagon Smith and the Martians" is set in the 1850s, and starts out in Missouri, and I tried to get every detail about Thomas "Windwagon" Smith as historically accurate as I could, but once he gets to Ray Bradbury's Mars (used with Mr. Bradbury's kind permission), all bets are off.

The places visited in "My Mother and I Go Shopping" are loosely based on the history of New England, but only *very* loosely.

"One Million Lightbulbs" is set in 1905 New York, and everything about Steeplechase Park and Dreamland and Luna Park is accurate, but Miracle Park never existed.

"Unicornucopia" takes place in an unspecified college town, "Best Present Ever!" in Arizona, "Jim Tuckerman's Angel" starts in Kentucky and winds up in Washington D.C.; "When Hell Froze Over" is, of course, set in Hell, and all of them take place roughly in the present day—but only roughly. They're deliberately not tied to any specific time.

"Three Days Late for the Hanging" nominally takes place in Colorado in the 1870s, but there is no pretense of accuracy whatsoever.

I honestly don't know where "The Girl Who Couldn't Fly" is set. When I started writing it I thought of it as post-apocalyptic, where the apocalypse was magical in nature, but I don't know if that's where it wound up—and I don't much care, either.

So here are ten stories that play fast and loose with history for the sake of fun. I had fun writing them, certainly, and I hope you'll have fun reading them.

Lawrence Watt-Evans

May 2011

Takoma Park, Maryland

Revised February 2023

Bainbridge Island, Washington

The Final Folly of Captain Dancy

1.

I was right there beside him when it happened, and I saw the whole thing. It wasn't anything but pure bad luck, such as could happen to anyone—but it had never happened to the captain before, and I'd guess he wasn't ready for it.

We had just come out of Old Joe's Tavern, where the captain had beaten the snot out of three young troublemakers, and we'd left by way of the alley, since the troublemakers had shipmates of their own, and that alleyway wasn't any too clean. I didn't see exactly what it was the captain stepped in, but it was brown and greasy, and when his foot hit it that foot went straight out from under him and he fell, and his head fetched up hard against the brick wall, and there was a snap like kindling broken across your knee, and there he was on the ground, dead.

It was pure bad luck, and the damnedest thing, but that's how it happened, and Captain Jack Dancy, who'd had three ships shot out from under him, who'd come through the battle of Cushgar Corners, where only three men survived, without a scratch, who'd sired bastards on half the wives in Collyport without ever a husband suspecting, who'd stolen the entire treasury from the Pundit of Oul and got away clean, who'd escaped from the Dungeon Pits of the Black Sorcerer on Little Hengist, who was the only man ever pardoned by Governor "Hangman" Lee, who'd climbed Dawson's Butte with only a bullwhip for tackle—that man, Jolly Jack Dancy, lay dead in the alley behind Old Joe's Tavern of a simple fall and a broken neck.

And that meant that me and the rest of the crew of the good ship *Bonny Anne* were in deep trouble.

We didn't know the half of it yet, of course, but even then, drunk as I was, I knew it wasn't good.

I saw him fall, and I heard his neck break, but I was muddled by drink, and I didn't really believe that the captain could die, like any other mortal, and most particularly not in such a stupid and easy fashion, so I judged that he was just hurt, and I picked him up and tried to get him to walk, but a corpse doesn't do much walking without at least a bit of a charm put on it, so then I swung him up across my shoulders and I headed down that alley, swaying slightly, and in a hurry to get back to the *Bonny Anne*, where either Doc Brewer or the captain's lady, Miss Melissa, could see about reviving him.

I think somewhere at the back of my mind I must have known he was dead, but sozzled as I was I probably thought even that wouldn't necessarily have been entirely permanent. I've seen my share of zombies, and I know they aren't of much use and don't remember a damned bit of what they knew in life, but I'd heard tales of other ways of dealing with the dead, one sort of necromancy or the other, and I won't call them lies as yet.

I had enough sense left to stay in the alleys as much as I could, and halfway to the docks I ran into Black Eddie driving a freight wagon, and I hailed him and threw the captain's carcass in the back, and then climbed up beside him.

It took me two or three tries to get up to the driver's bench, what with the liquor in me, but I made it eventually, and Black Eddie had us rolling before I had my ass on the plank.

"Head for the ship," I told him, and he nodded, as he was already bound that way. He snapped the reins and sped the horses a mite.

Then he threw a look behind him, and turned to me.

"Billy," he said, "what's wrong wi' the Captain?"

"Broke his fool neck," said I.

He looked at me startled, then looked back at that corpse, and then asked, "You mean he's dead?"

I started to nod, and then to shrug, and then I said, "Damned if I know, Eddie, but I'm afraid so."

"Damme!" Eddie said, and he flicked the reins again for more speed.

That brought our situation to my attention. "Eddie," said I, looking around in puzzlement, "What're ye doing with this wagon?"

"Damned if *I* know, Billy," he said. "'Twas the captain's order that I get it, and have it at the docks by midnight, but he didn't think to tell me why."

"Oh," I said, trying to remember if the captain had said anything about a wagon, and not managing to recall much of anything at all. The captain had mostly been on about the usual, whiskey and women and the woes of the world, and hadn't spoken much of any special plans. A moment or two later we rolled out onto the dock where the *Bonny Anne* lay, and I hadn't come up with a thing.

"Well," I said, "Mr. Abernathy will know."

We'd tied up right to the dock, as the harbor in Collyport is a good and deep one, with a drop-off as steep as a ship-chandler's prices; no need to ride out at anchor and come in with the boats, as there would be in most of the ports we traded in. About a dozen ships were in port, at one place or another, and the *Bonny Anne* was one of them, right there at hand, and we could see the lads aboard her watching as we came riding up.

Looking up at them, the thought came to me that perhaps there were things we had best keep to ourselves, at least until we'd had a chance to talk matters over with our first mate, Lieutenant John Hastings Abernathy, who had the watch aboard and was Captain Dancy's closest confidant. It seemed to me I recalled a few things I hadn't before.

"Eddie," said I, "Give me a hand with the captain, would you? And let on he's just drunk, or been clouted, and let's not say any more of it than we must, shall we?"

He gave me the fish-eye, but then he shrugged. "What the hell, then," he said. "Let it be Mr. Abernathy what spreads the news, if you like."

"It'd suit me," I said. I was thinking of a deal the captain had made, six years before, with the Caliburn Witch.

So the two of us hauled that corpse out of the wagon with a bit more care than was honestly called for, and we got it upright between us, me with my hand at the back of the head so the crew would not be seeing it loll off to one side too badly, and we walked up the gangplank with the feet dragging between us, and we headed straight back to the captain's cabin.

Old Wheeler, the captain's man, was pottering about, and we shooed him away and dumped poor old Jack Dancy's mortal remains on the bunk, and then Black Eddie sent me to fetch Mr. Abernathy.

I found Hasty Bernie on the quarterdeck, just where he should have been, and had little doubt in my mind that he'd watched us every inch from the wagon to the break in the poop, but he didn't let on a bit, he just watched me walk up, and stood there silent as a taut sail until I said, "Permission to speak, sir?"

"Go ahead, Mr. Jones," he said, and I knew we were being formal, as he didn't call me Billy, but I didn't quite see why, as yet.

"Mr. Abernathy," I said, "I'd like a word with you in private, if I might, regardin' the captain."

He lifted up on his toes, with his hands behind his back, the way he always did when he was nervous about something, and he said, "And what is it that you can't say right here, Mr. Jones? Who's to hear you?"

I wasn't happy to hear that, at all. He must have thought I was getting out of line somehow, and I remembered as he'd asked me especially to keep a close eye on some of the men, as they might be thinking the captain wasn't looking out for them proper.

I wasn't too concerned about mutiny brewing, not just then, in particular as I *had* been keeping an eye out, and hadn't seen a man aboard who didn't have faith in the captain. They might not think much of the rest of us, but they all admired the captain and trusted in him to do right by them.

Which made my news that much worse. "Mr. Abernathy," said I, "you know as well as I do that any word said on this deck can be heard by any as might care to listen from below the rail, either on the halfdeck or on the docks, be they crewmen or townsfolk or any others that might chance by, not even mentionin' the possibilities of sorcery and black magic as might be involved. You were with the captain at Little Hengist, weren't you?"

He blinked at me, and looked about as if he expected to see the Sorcerer's creatures climbing up the rigging, and then he turned back to me and said, "Very well, Mr. Jones, lead the way, then."

I led him straight to the cabin, where the poor captain's body lay and Black Eddie stood guard, and we closed up the sliding trap on the skylight above the map table, and we checked the stern windows and made sure they were tight, and Black Eddie went from one cabinet to the next and made sure that there was nobody tucked away in any of them, neither a crewman tucked small nor the Sorcerer's homunculi, not as we really thought the Sorcerer still gave a tinker's dam for any of us aboard the *Bonny Anne*, but you never know.

And when we were sure that the place was as private as we could make it, I turned to Hasty Bernie and said, "He's dead."

The night air on the ride down to the ship, and the business of getting the corpse aboard and getting ourselves alone and private with Bernie had given my head time to clear, and there wasn't any doubt any more. I'd heard that snap I'd heard, and I knew it for what it was.

Bernie snapped his head around like to break his own neck and stared at that lump on the bunk. "Dead?" he said, "Captain Dancy?"

"Dead as a stone," Black Eddie said. "Whilst Billy was fetchin' you down, I took a look at 'im, and listened for his heart and felt for his pulse, and the man's dead if ever a man was."

"Good Lord," Bernie said, staring at the corpse. "Now what are we going to do?"

I blinked, and looked at Black Eddie, who looked back at me.

"We were hopin'," Eddie pointed out to Bernie, "that *you* could tell *us* that."

"Me?" Bernie looked from one of us to the other and back, with a look on him as if we'd just suggested he bugger the Governor's pet penguin.

"You *are* in command," Eddie said mildly.

Bernie looked at us each, desperately, and then crossed to the bunk and knelt. "You're *sure* he's dead?" he asked.

We both nodded, but Bernie bent down and checked for himself, feeling for a breath from the nose and mouth, listening for the heart, feeling for a pulse, and finding nothing at all.

It was just then that someone knocked at the cabin door, and we looked at one another like as we were schoolboys caught with the maid and her bloomers down, and Black Eddie stared at Hasty

Bernie, and Hasty Bernie stared around the room, and after a moment I called, "Who is it?"

"Got a letter for the captain," someone answered.

"Slip it under the door," I said.

The fellow hesitated, and then said, "I don't think I can do that, sir; I was told to give it to Captain Dancy and no other, or it'd be my neck in a noose."

I glanced at the others, but they just shrugged, so I went to the door and opened it.

There stood Jamie McPhee, with the letter in his hand, and I saw the red seal upon it and knew it wasn't just a bill from the chandler nor any such trifle.

"The Captain's ill," I said. "Got a clout on the head in a fight, and that atop a bottle of bad rum, and he's in no shape for readin' a letter. If you'd care to come in and put it in his hand, you'll have done as you were told, but you needn't wait for him to wake; he's dead to the world, and it might be noon before he rises again."

Or it might be Judgment Day, I added to myself.

The boy looked past me at the body on the bunk, and the situation seemed mighty plain, so he shrugged and said, "Well, I done my best, Mr. Jones, and with both you here and Mr. Abernathy there watching I reckon it's right enough. Here's the letter then, and I'm shut of it." And he handed me the letter.

Parchment, it was.

Jamie hurried off, and I closed the door tight and took the letter to Hasty Bernie.

I held it out to him, but he looked at it as if it were a hungry piranha, and at me as if I were straight out of Bedlam. "That's for the Captain," he said.

"And that's you, sir," I said. "Seein' as Captain Dancy's dead."

He stared at it for a moment longer, and I stood there, waiting.

"Oh, all right, damn you," he said, and he snatched the letter away and looked at it.

His face went white.

"Oh, Lord," he said. "It's from Governor Lee."

"Open it," Black Eddie said. "Let's hear the worst."

2.

His hands shaking, Bernie broke the big red seal and opened it, and he read it aloud, and what it said was this:

"Dear Captain Dancy, As you will recall as well as do I, when I granted you Pardon for your Crimes this three years past, there were certain Terms agreed upon by us both. Though we have not always seen eye to eye on every Detail, I have, I feel, fully lived up to my end of the Arrangement, and I confess you have done well enough on your own. However, one Provision of our Agreement remains in Doubt. You must surely know to what I refer. Having seen Mistress Coyne twice this fortnight past, how could you not? I trust you will remedy this Oversight forthwith. Should you fail to satisfy me of your good Will by this coming Dawn, either by completing our Arrangement or by suitably demonstrating your Intent, I fear I will be required to consider the entire Agreement void, your Pardon revoked, and your Ship forfeit to the Crown. Signed, Geo. Lee, Governor."

When he'd read that, Bernie stared at the paper for a long moment. Then he looked up at Eddie and at me, and said, "Good Christ, whatever is *this* about?"

Eddie and me, we shook our heads, as we hadn't either of us any more idea than a duck.

"Who's this Mistress Coyne, then?" Eddie asked.

"I have no idea," Bernie said.

"Nor do I," said I.

"An' what do we do *now*?" Eddie asked.

"Your ship forfeit to the crown, it says," I remarked. "Seems to me that we'd want to avoid that. I'm not overly concerned about losing the Captain's pardon, as that was for a sentence of death, and he's clear of that, but I'm not eager to lose the ship."

"Could he take it?" Bernie asked thoughtfully. "We've men and guns, after all. We could fight."

"Aye, that we could," I said. "But we'd lose. The Governor's got men and guns himself, aboard the frigate just across the harbor."

"The *Armistead Castle*," Bernie said. "I'd forgot her."

"Aye," I said. "That's the one."

"And the *Castle*'s ready for sea," Eddie pointed out. "I saw meself, they've a full crew aboard, standing a proper watch tonight, not a port watch."

"The Governor must ha' meant that to fright the Captain," I said. "He's lettin' us know he's serious in his threats."

"I don't know about the Captain, but it frightens me right well," Hasty Bernie said. "That frigate's sixteen guns a side; we couldn't possibly stand up to her."

"Aye," Eddie said. "Well then, shall we fetch the men and raise anchor to run? We can be over the horizon by dawn, if we're brisk about it."

"Nay," said I, "for then we'd be fugitives, and shut of Collyport forever, not to mention having all the rest of the Royal Navy after us."

"Well, and aren't we fugitives now?" Eddie asked.

"Not here," said I. "Not with the governor's pardon."

"But that runs out at dawn," Eddie said.

"Not if we show our good intent," I told him.

Bernie was still staring at the parchment, but he said, "Maybe if we just went to the governor and told him what happened..."

"Would he believe us?" I asked.

"We've got the bloody corpse to prove it, ye blidget!" Eddie said. "How could he not?"

"Are ye plannin' to drag the captain all the way up to the governor's palace, then, and haul it in with us when he agrees to see us—*if* he agrees to see us?"

Black Eddie had to think about that one for a moment.

"We might could try it," he said at last, but we knew by the tone that his heart weren't in it. I was ready to mention the Caliburn Witch, and her promise to live and let live only until she heard that Jack Dancy was dead, but I could see Eddie wasn't going to argue, so I held off.

"Why'd the governor want to be so bloody cryptic in his letter, anyway?" Bernie snapped.

"And why'd the captain not tell us what in hell he wanted with that wagon, and what he'd promised the governor?" Black Eddie retorted.

"And when," said I, "Did the captain *ever* tell us what he was up to?"

That silenced them both, for the truth was that Jack Dancy had always been close with his counsel. As he told me once, "Billy," he said, "if you don't tell people what you're planning, they won't worry about what might go wrong." And sure enough, he'd always pulled off everything he'd put his hand to, no matter how bad it looked, no matter how bad it *was*, he'd always pulled it off. Sometimes he only survived by the skin of his teeth, but he always survived, as if all the gods of luck owed him heavily and had interest to pay.

Well, his luck had run out tonight.

And we were standing there looking at one another, the three of us, when the cabin door opened. We heard the hinges creak, and the three of us spun about, and Black Eddie's dirk was out, and my own hand seemed to be on the hilt of me own dagger, and there we all were, staring at Miss Melissa, who was by her face just as surprised to see us as we were to see her.

"Good evenin' to ye, gentlemen," she said, "Is the captain in?"

Eddie and I looked at one another, and then at Hasty Bernie, who swallowed and said, "Miss Melissa, there's bad news."

"Oh? Is he drunk, Mr. Abernathy?" She looked at the body on the bunk and stepped into the cabin.

Bernie looked at the two of us, but we were no help to him, and his face twisted up. "Worse," he said.

Miss Melissa gave him a look such as I hope I never have to endure. "He's hurt, then?" she asked, closing the door behind her.

"Dead," said Black Eddie.

"*Dead?*" She was at the bunk before I could blink, tipping the corpse's head back for a good look.

For a moment, we all just stood and watched her, as she saw what we'd all seen. Then she let out a great sob.

"*Damn* you, Jack Dancy!" she said, her back still to us, and her voice weren't steady at all, "What the hell did you go and die for? Eddie, go get Doc Brewer—he was down in the after hold last I saw, counting those masks we got at Pennington's Cay."

Black Eddie threw a look at Hasty Bernie, who nodded, and then Eddie trotted out the door.

Miss Melissa turned, and we could see the tears running down her face, and it seemed I felt my own throat thickening and my eyes going damp. All that strong drink must have numbed me, a bit, for surely the captain's death was enough to make a man cry, but it wasn't until I saw Miss Melissa weeping that it came home to me.

"How did it happen, Billy?" she asked me.

I shrugged, and said, "He fell. Hit his head on a brick wall, and his neck snapped."

She stared at me, and the tears stopped.

"That's *all?*" she asked.

I nodded. "That's all," I said.

"That son of a bitch!" she said. "You mean it wasn't the Governor's men? Nor the Sorcerer? Nor the Pundit? Nor the *Amber Lassie*? Nor 'Tholomew Sanchez?"

"No," I said. "Wasn't any of those. He slipped and fell while drunk, and that's all there was to it."

"Well, I'll... a man like Jack Dancy, dead like that?"

I nodded.

"That's not fitting. It's a damn poor ending to a life like that!"

"I'd agree with that," I said, and Bernie nodded.

For a moment the three of us stood silent, thinking about the captain. It was Miss Melissa who broke the quiet.

"What were his last words, then?" she asked me. "Did he leave us with a fine speech to remember him?"

I had to think about that. We'd been in Old Joe's, and we'd just beaten those sailors and were on our way out through the back, and Jack Dancy had turned to me, smiling and drunk.

"His last words," I said, "were, 'Billy, I'm going to need five guineas later tonight; have you got 'em?'"

Miss Melissa glared at me like as I'd belched in church. "That's a hell of a way to go out, asking for money!"

I didn't argue any. Instead, I said, "I think there's something you'd best be seein', Miss Melissa." I pointed to the governor's letter.

Bernie handed it to her, and she read it, and then she looked up and asked, "Who's Mistress Coyne?"

"We don't know," I said. "That's just what we were askin' amongst ourselves when you came in."

She squinted at me suspiciously, and I looked her in the eye because I wasn't doing anything but telling the simple truth. "D'ye think Jack was bedding her?" she asked me.

I shrugged. "I don't know, Miss Melissa," I said, "I truly don't. I never heard her name until this letter arrived, not half an hour ago."

"Miss Melissa," Bernie said, "while I understand your concern with the mysterious Mistress Coyne, might I point out that it's rather more urgent that we discover just what promises Captain Dancy had made to Governor Lee, than whether he'd been... ah..."

"Than whether he'd been tomcatting about again," she finished for him. "You mean you don't *know* what the promise was?"

"No," Bernie said.

She looked at me, and I shook my head.

"Nor I," I said.

"Well," she said, looking at the letter, "We can't ask the governor, for he'd not have the likes of us in his palace."

I threw Bernie a glance, and shook my head as he started to open his mouth. There was no need for her to know that we'd been in the palace half a dozen times with Jack Dancy, going in by way of the caves round the other side of Collins Island that led into the wine cellars. Nor did she need to be told that Captain Dancy had once walked in the front gate at the governor's invitation. The circumstances for that one didn't bear telling to the captain's lady.

"So that means we'll have to see this Mistress Coyne," Miss Melissa announced.

I blinked.

"Beggin' your pardon," I said, "but how are we to do that? We don't know who she is, or where, and we've no more than five hours to dawn, I'd judge, when the governor's said the ship's to be forfeit."

"Well," Miss Melissa said, "It seems plain to me that *somebody* knows who she is and where she's to be found. You tell me that you two don't know, but someone aboard might—did Jack go alone when he saw her, without word to any? And even if he did, there's the governor who knows who and where she is, and the governor's spies who told him that Jack had been to see her; can't we ask them?"

"Well, we can't ask the governor, can we?" I said.

"And half the crew's out carousing," Bernie pointed out.

"Well, then, what about the governor's spies?" Miss Melissa asked.

I had to think about that. Something seemed familiar there.

"Mr. Abernathy," I said, speakin' slowly so as to think about what I was saying, "wa'n't it one of the governor's men what brought you that bottle on Sunday?"

The bottle I referred to had had an imp in it once, and the captain had wanted it for a deal he was making with the vengeful brother of the harbormaster's first wife, but that's beside the point.

"Aye," Hasty Bernie said. "It was. What of it?"

Miss Melissa looked at me. "D'you think, then, that this man might know where we can find the wench?"

I shrugged. "He might, and what better have we got to do, than to ask him?"

"D'you know where he's to be found, then?" she asked.

"No," I said. "But I know who does."

It was at that moment that Black Eddie flung open the door and stepped in, with Doc Brewer close on his heels—and Peter Long the bo'sun right behind Doc Brewer.

"Here, you can't come in!" Bernie called at Peter. "The captain's ill!"

"Oh," Peter said, taking in the lump on the bunk and noticing who he was following. He stopped with his toes on the sill. "Well, then, tell the captain I've got his parrot."

Hasty Bernie blinked in surprise, and Miss Melissa stared, and I asked, "*What* parrot?"

"The one he sent me after, Billy. He told me to go up to the Hightown Market and buy the big parrot from the one-eyed bugger in the red and gold tent, and I did, and I've got the damn bird in the fo'c'sle, and it like to bit me nose off."

"All right, Peter," said I, "If he didn't hear that himself I'll be sure to tell him, you've my word on it."

"Thank ye, Billy. I've no fancy to keep the bird myself." He tipped his cap, and turned away.

Black Eddie and Doc Brewer had been standing in the cabin listening to this, and when Peter was gone and Doc was closing the cabin door, Black Eddie said, "A *parrot?*"

"I've no more of it than you, Eddie," I said.

"Doctor," Miss Melissa said, paying no attention to Eddie and myself, "the captain's dead, and there's no doubt of it, so it's not your medical skills that we wanted. It's necromancy, and you're the man aboard that knows most of magicks, so I sent for you."

"Dead?" Doc Brewer started, and turned to the bunk.

"Yes, he's dead, damn him!" Miss Melissa snapped, with her hands on her hips and fire in her eye. A pretty thing, she was then.

"Miss Melissa..." Bernie started to say, but at a glare from her he thought better of it.

Doc Brewer wasn't listening. He was inspecting Jack Dancy's remains, poking at the neck with his fingers and muttering to himself.

"Whacked his head, he did," he said. "Snapped the third cervical vertebra, and the severed edge went right through the spinal cord, by the look of it. He probably never felt a thing."

That was some comfort to me, hearing that.

Doc muttered on for a moment, whilst the rest of us gradually lost interest in talking and got to watching and listening. Finally, Doc straightened up and said, "He may not even know he's dead, it was so quick. If that's the fact, then the chances are good that his ghost is still back where he died, trying to ascertain what's happened to him. A witch might be able to locate the spirit and converse with it, but earthbound souls aren't anything I can handle."

Miss Melissa started to protest, but Doc Brewer held up a hand to silence her. "On the other hand," he said, "Jack Dancy was a sharp man, and a realist, and he may have seen what happened and know he's dead. In that case, there's no telling what's become of him, whether he's earthbound or on to his final rest or somewhere in between. If he's yet in limbo, I can bespeak him, and if he's in hell, which I pray he's not, for rogue that he was I liked the man and I thought well of him...well, if he's in hell, I may be able to reach him but it's not sure. If he's gone to the reward of the blessed, alas, though *he'll* be happy, *we* won't, for if that's the case he's beyond all earthly concerns and can't be reached by any means known to mortal man save direct divine intercession—and I've no knack for that, let me tell you! The Pope himself can't rely on it!"

Hasty Bernie snorted. "Of course he can't," he said, "He's an old fraud, no holier than I am, and his whole church..." He caught sight of our faces and stopped.

Black Eddie's a Papist, of course, and we all knew it, and Hasty Bernie had no call to speak ill of the Bishop of Rome in front of Eddie that way, but his own faith had got the better of him for a moment.

We didn't hold it against him, though, and Miss Melissa carried on, asking the doc, "So you might be able to reach him and ask him what his agreement with the governor was?"

Doc was puzzled by that. "The governor?"

Miss Melissa handed him the letter, and he read it.

"I don't know," he said, handing it back, "but I'll see what I can do. I'd best prepare my spells—the sooner the better."

We could none of us argue with that, so we stood politely as the doc left.

When the door closed behind him, Miss Melissa turned to me and said, "You were sayin' that you can find the governor's man, who might lead us to this Mistress Coyne?"

"Not I," I replied, "but Jamie McPhee, as he handles errands like that for the captain."

"Let's get on with it, then," she said. "Have him in here and get *on* with it!"

"Couldn't we wait until the doctor..." Bernie began, but Miss Melissa cut him off with a glare.

"Now, Mr. Abernathy," I said, "You heard what Doc Brewer told us; it's as like as not he can't contact the captain. And we've no time to waste in trying. Eddie, can ye call the lad?"

Black Eddie nodded and stepped out, and the rest of us stood about fiddling our thumbs, staring each at the other and thinking on what we should do.

3.

We had none of us come up with anything when Jamie arrived, of himself, without a sign of Black Eddie. We sent him to talk to the governor's man and find out who this Mistress Coyne might be.

" Why?" he asked.

Hasty Bernie started to say, "Well, lad, the Captain..."

Miss Melissa hushed him. "It's not your concern, boy," she said, "and we've no time to explain. You just go and ask, and come back here quick!"

He nodded, and hurried out.

We all looked after him as he left. Hasty Bernie remarked, "Collyport's a rough place by night; I hope he'll have no problems."

"Ah, the lad knows the town," I said, "There's nothing to worry about."

"Nothing to worry about!" Hasty Bernie shouted, glaring at me. "The Governor's about to claim the ship, the captain's dead, and not one of us even knows what's happening, and you'd tell us not to worry?"

"Well," I said, "and what good did worry ever do a man? There's naught more to be done until we hear from the lad or Doc Brewer, is there? Then there's nothing *we* can do, and no reason to worry!"

"An odd philosophy," Hasty Bernie said.

"A fool's philosophy," Miss Melissa retorted. "How do we know there's naught can be done? What if the doctor can't reach the captain, nor the boy find this Mistress Coyne? Are we to give up the ship without a fight, and starve in the streets?"

"Oh, we'd not starve," I said. "A man who'd sailed with Jack Dancy can surely find another berth! But I'd as soon keep the ship, I'll agree with that."

"Is it ours to keep, though?" Hasty Bernie asked, suddenly thoughtful. "Did the captain own it? Who are his heirs?"

"*We* are," Miss Melissa snapped. "Who else could there be?"

"I thought his family," Bernie began. "His children..."

"*What* family?" Miss Melissa shouted. "He swore he'd never married!"

"Nor did he," I told her.

"Then what children?" she demanded triumphantly.

"Miss Melissa," I said, "you must know better than that. By last count he knew of thirty-one, he told me this Sunday past, and he's been the sole support of the seven whose mothers aren't presently married. And there's a sister back in Weymouth, the captain spoke of her often—she's married to a chandler by the name of Wiggins, I understand."

Her mouth fell open and she stared wide-eyed at me.

"I suppose that Mrs. Wiggins would be the heir of record," Bernie said, "given the lack of a marriage. But did Captain Dancy truly own the ship himself, or did he have a backer?"

"Thirty-one?" Miss Melissa squeaked.

"Or thereabouts," I told her. "You'll understand, the captain often took the lass's word, and I'll not swear they were all of them entirely truthful. But then he may have missed a few, as well, so I'd judge as it might balance out."

"*Thirty-one bastards?*" she shrieked at me.

"Or thereabouts," I repeated.

She stared at me, and Hasty Bernie asked, "Do you think Mrs. Wiggins would know if there were a backer? I'll need to send her a letter in any case, so I thought..."

"*Who cares?*" Miss Melissa screamed, turning to Bernie. "Who cares about any sister, or backer, or the thirty-one bleeding bastards that son of a bitch left? *We're* the ones who *have* the ship, and I don't intend to let the Governor or anybody else take it away! Call the men to their stations—we'll take this ship out and sink anyone who tries to stop us!"

I looked at Bernie, but he was looking helplessly back at me. "Miss Melissa," I said, "I don't want to lose the *Bonny Anne* any more than you do, nor will we if we can help it, but there's no need for all that, now. The doc's trying to bespeak the captain, and Jamie's gone to find us Mistress Coyne, and there's still a fine hope that we'll be able to keep the Governor's pardon *and* the ship, safe here in Collyport. If ye must do *something*, you'd be better to see if you can think what the Captain promised the Governor, not sending the men to stations."

"Well said, Mr. Jones," Hasty Bernie said. "Though I still think that determining the ship's rightful owner..."

"Can wait," I said, interrupting him. "Whoever owns her surely won't be wantin' her forfeit to the Crown, and if we can hold her free we'll be in a position to bargain when the time comes. First, though, we've to hold her free."

"Aye," Bernie admitted.

"And to do that, we've to know what the Governor wants."

"Or to get out of Collyport," Miss Melissa said.

"And go where?" I asked her, as sweetly as I could. "In a ship forfeit to the Crown, every English-speakin' port will be closed to us as fast as the word can reach them—and every *other* port is *already* closed to the *Bonny Anne!*"

"All right, then," she said, "What does the Governor want?"

"I've no idea," I admitted, "But the Captain did, and he'd made arrangements, it seems."

"What arrangements?" she asked.

"Well," I told her, "Black Eddie was to have a freight wagon at the ship by midnight, and it's there on the dock now. Peter Long was to fetch a particular parrot, and he's got it in the fo'c'sle. It might be there are other things as well that I've not happened on yet."

"A freight wagon?"

I nodded. I didn't mention that we'd used it to fetch the captain's corpse in.

"And a parrot?"

I nodded again.

There was a knock at the door.

We looked at one another, and then Miss Melissa called, "Come in!"

The door opened, and there was Black Eddie with a scrawny little ape of a man I'd never clapped eyes on before. Before Eddie could speak, the stranger barked at us, "If ye'd changed yer damned plans, ye might 'a' had the courtesy to ha' told me!"

"See here, man," Hasty Bernie said, "Who are you talking to that way?"

"I'm talkin' to *you*, ye pompous twit," he sputtered, "You and yer damned captain, what told me to wait for 'is bloody signal that was due at midnight and he ain't gimme yet! And there he is, sleepin' off a bottle or two, ain't he? Damned if I shouldn't 'a' known it. Bloody idiot. Bloody hell!"

He turned and would have stamped away, save that Black Eddie was in his way, which gave Miss Melissa time to ask, "What signal?"

The stranger turned back and squinted at her, then snapped, "A red light on the mizzen. Didn't the damned fool tell ye?"

She shook her head, and Bernie and I just stood there.

The little man looked over at the captain's mortal remains and snorted. "Reckon he passed out before he got that far. Well, then, d'ye want me to fire that warehouse, or don't ye?"

Bernie and I looked at each other. Miss Melissa started to ask, "*What* warehouse?" but I tapped her shoulder before she'd got a good start on the second word, and she hushed up nicely.

"We're runnin' a little late tonight," I said. "As ye said yourself, the captain's been no help to us." I looked at Bernie.

"Aye, if you could bear with us yet for awhile, we'd appreciate it," he said.

The little man looked us all over and was about to snort again when I said, "Listen, man, you go back to your post and gi' us ten more minutes beyond. If the red light's not up by then, belay the whole job and go home to your bed with our blessings. There's an extra silver guinea for your trouble. Fair enough?" I fished the coin from me purse and held it up. Didn't leave me much, but he didn't look the sort to settle for a shilling.

He squinted again, then said, "Fair enough. Hand it over."

I obliged him, and he tucked the guinea away, and Black Eddie led him back to the rail.

Miss Melissa watched him over the side, then slammed the door and spun on us.

"What in hell was *that* about?" she asked.

Hasty Bernie shrugged.

"Seems to me," I said, "as the captain had a diversion planned. A big one. And I'll wager I know what warehouse it is, too, as Jack Dancy was always a man to get the most for his efforts."

Bernie blinked. Miss Melissa stared at me for a moment, and then a smile spread across her face.

"Sanchez?" she asked.

I nodded. "He's out to sea now, but he's got a good lot of his booty tucked away where he didn't figure it to be shot up if he meets an unfriendly ship. Wasn't worth our while doin' a thing to it in the ordinary course, but if it's a diversion we need anyway, why, there 'tis ready to go."

"But what do we need a diversion *for*?" Bernie asked, his face troubled.

"I don't know," I said, "But we have ten minutes to decide whether we need one at all."

"If Jack arranged it, we'll probably need it," Miss Melissa said, and I had to agree that that was generally true.

"There's a freight wagon," I said. "And this letter from the Governor, and visits to Mistress Coyne, and now a fire to be set as a diversion just as the freight wagon was to be here."

"And a parrot," Bernie added.

"And a bloody damn parrot," I agreed. "With all that, then, does either of you have any notion of just what might be goin' on?"

They looked at each other, and then back at me.

"No," Bernie said.

"Seems to me," I said slowly, "that a diversion over at the warehouse is meant to draw attention away from the ship. If it were a diversion elsewhere that the captain wanted, he could have made it himself ready enough right here, or any number of ways."

"If it really *is* a diversion," Miss Melissa suggested.

I considered that, while Bernie protested, "Captain Dancy wouldn't burn down that warehouse just for spite! And why on a signal from the ship, if he just wanted it done?"

"Maybe not a *diversion*," I said, "so much as *cover*. Now, the captain must have planned on being here aboard ship at midnight, so as to give the signal, and to do whatever was to be done with the freight wagon. Suppose that you're aboard your ship, and you see a fire over there on the great wharf—what do you do?"

"I put out to sea, of course," Bernie said. "To get clear of sparks."

"D'ye think, then, that Jack was going to run?" Miss Melissa asked. "He was no coward!"

I shook my head. "No, not Jack Dancy. He wouldn't ha' run from Governor Lee, nor from the *Armistead Castle*, nor from the devils of Hell. Nor would he give up Collyport so easy. So if he'd knowed what the Governor was on about in that letter, and that this was the night he had to deliver, he'd ha' done his damnedest to deliver. So he planned on doing it from the sea, somehow."

"What about the wagon?" Bernie asked. "Maybe he figured on sending the ship to sea, so that everyone would think he was gone, and all the while he'd be about his business with the wagon."

"No, Mr. Abernathy," I said, "for then he'd want the *Bonny Anne*'s departure noted, and he'd 'a' had us sail out in broad daylight, not put out at midnight to escape a fire. No, the fire's to give us a reason for leaving harbor at night, I'm sure of it."

I had an idea, then, of where the captain might have had in mind to go, but I didn't know the why of it yet at all.

There'd be no point in leaving at midnight if we were to be bound for another island; we couldn't reach another that night, and if we'd a need to reach another at a particular time it would be easier to make the time right along the way than by sailing out in the dark—even in a harbor we knew as well as that one, sailing out at night is a bit of a risk.

So we were going somewhere else on Collins Island, somewhere that was best reached by sea, and where he didn't want us to be seen, and where we *would* have been seen if we'd sailed there by day, and somewhere that wasn't close enough to row there easy in the ship's launch.

I knew what that meant, plain enough. The captain had meant to sail around to the caves.

But why?

If he'd meant to meet with someone there, then we were bound to miss it entirely, as it was more than an hour after midnight and we hadn't even got most of the crew aboard, as far as I knew.

But then, if someone was waiting in the caves for us, he weren't about to go much of anywhere in any hurry, as the cliffs above and to the sides were a mighty rough climb, and the cliff below led nowhere but the sea.

There was the other end of the cave, of course, but there weren't many as knew about that.

All the same, if we were to have met someone there, he might be there yet by the time we could reach him, or he might not, and I'd have been much happier if I'd have known just what to expect.

I wished as Jamie McPhee would hurry back.

Someone knocked at the door, and I thought as my wish had been granted, but then Black Eddie called from without, "It's been nigh on ten minutes."

"Aye," I said, and then I called, "Send up the signal! And prepare for sea!" Boldness, Captain Dancy used to tell me, boldness will win sooner than wit.

"*What?*" Miss Melissa shrieked at me, and I looked at her quite reproachful, as it hurt my ear.

"Mr. Jones," Bernie said, "Billy, do you know just what you're doing?"

"Not entirely," I confessed, "But I have a fair to middlin' idea."

"What about Jamie?" Miss Melissa asked, still shouting, but not half as loud.

"I'll send a man to fetch him," Bernie said.

"I'd not waste the time," I said. "Beggin' your pardon, Mr. Abernathy. But what you might do is put a boat over, and leave it by the dock with a couple of men aboard, to row the lad out to us when he arrives."

Bernie stared at me thoughtful for a moment, then nodded, and he left the cabin to see to it.

That left me, and Miss Melissa, and the corpse, and when I realized I was the only living man there with her my tongue dried out and of a sudden I found nothing to say.

She hadn't the same problem, though.

"And who do you think you are, Billy Jones, to be ordering about Mr. Abernathy and doing what you please?"

"I'm second mate of this ship, Miss Melissa," I answered her, "And I'm just doin' what I can to see us all safe, now that the captain's not here to do it."

She looked me in the eye for a moment, and I didn't blink. Then she turned away and looked at the captain's body and whispered, "Damn you, Jack Dancy!"

Then she turned again and marched out.

4.

I covered up the captain and tried to make him look natural, just in case someone should chance to look in, and as I was about to go up on deck there was old Wheeler coming in, about to whine about somewhat or the other, and thinking quick I held up a finger to hush him.

"The Captain's bad tonight," I told him. "Don't you touch him, unless you want to kiss the gratings tomorrow!"

Wheeler nodded, and went about his business, throwing a glance over his shoulder every so oft, but not going near the corpse.

I just hoped the captain wouldn't start to stink too soon. Maybe Doc Brewer could do something about that.

Then I went up, and at first I thought that dawn was breaking and we'd wasted the whole night, but then I saw as this light was orange, and not the pink of dawn at all, and I realized as it was the warehouse on fire.

Around us, other ships were casting off, their crews running about and shouting. I could see the *Armistead Castle* spreading canvas already— she had a good crew, that ship.

And there aboard the *Bonny Anne* about me were the men and boys hanging in the rigging and watching the fire, and chattering amongst themselves like so many gulls, and the ship still at the dock!

I looked about and saw Hasty Bernie on the quarterdeck, staring up the streets of Collyport, and I was as angry with him as I'd ever been. "Hey!" I called. "You bloody damn fools, that's a fire over there, and there'll be sparks in the air, and our sails could catch! Cast off! Get us out to sea!"

I saw Peter Long throw a look at Hasty Bernie, but Bernie just nodded, and a moment later we were making way, pulling away from Collyport on the westerly airs.

I saw that at least Bernie had put down a boat, with Black Eddie in it, lest Jamie should happen along. And I saw that those other ships were putting out, as well—the *Bonny Anne* would be second or third out of the harbor, behind the *Armistead Castle* and maybe a merchantman off to starboard.

And the sparks *were* blowing in the wind and coming after us, and I didn't like it at all, and as I called the orders to work the sails I made sure to send a boy below for buckets and lines. It was just like the captain, to have come up with a diversion that could burn the ship!

It was only when we were safe out at sea that I took the time to think about anything but getting the *Bonny Anne* clear, and looked about.

There was Bernie on the quarterdeck—as I was myself, I noticed, having come up and taken the wheel without thinking about it. Miss Melissa was beside Hasty Bernie, and the two of them were arguing in whispers—I didn't trouble myself about just why, as yet. The rest of the crew, those as were aboard, were going about their business as they should, despite it being the middle of the night and near as black as the Sorcerer's soul.

Now it seemed to me as the time had come to decide what to do. The captain's plan called for sailing around the island to the caves, I was sure, but did we really want to do that?

Well, I supposed we did, as why else were we at sea?

I looked over at Mr. Abernathy and the captain's lady and decided that I'd best not bother them about it, as it would only mean more argument. I turned the wheel and put her on the starboard tack.

She was turning sweetly when I heard a hail from the masthead.

Our boat was coming out from the harbor, with Jamie McPhee and Black Eddie and, the lookout swore, a woman in the bow.

"Heave to," I called, "and bring 'em aboard!"

The men went to it with a will, and that boat seemed to skim right up to us in a mighty pretty piece of rowing, so it wasn't but a few minutes before we had the boat up out of the water and Jamie and Eddie and the woman on the halfdeck.

And sure enough they had a woman with them, a tall, comely thing, with red hair free to her waist and wearing a red and gold gown to go with it. She had a wide-brimmed red velvet hat on her head, with a veil all around, and white gloves to her hands, which seemed a little more than was purely necessary for the weather.

I called the orders to get us under way again whilst Jamie and Eddie brought her up to the quarterdeck. They took her over to Hasty Bernie, as he was the senior officer aboard, but I caught Eddie's eye and gestured for him to take the wheel.

"We're bound for the caves," I whispered to him. "Fast as we can get there without riskin' the rocks."

He nodded and grabbed the spokes, and I slipped over toward the others.

"Mr. Abernathy," Jamie was saying, "This is Mistress Annabelle Coyne."

Hasty Bernie took her hand and bowed, and smiled his best formal smile, and then stood there staring at her and looking stupid. 'Twas plain to me that the poor man had no idea what to do. I thought back on the watchbill and realized that he'd most likely been without sleep for nigh onto thirty hours, while I hadn't missed but an hour or two's sleep as yet, so I stepped forward.

I smiled and tipped my hat, once I remembered I was wearing it, as it happens I was, and said, "I'm Billy Jones, Mistress Coyne. Welcome aboard the *Bonny Anne*."

I could see Miss Melissa out of the corner of my eye, and she looked somewhat put out, both with Bernie and myself, but I didn't worry about that as yet.

"Thank you, Mr. Jones," said Mistress Coyne.

"My apologies, Mistress Coyne," Bernie said, "It seems I need Mr. Jones to remind me of my manners. Welcome, indeed, and thank you for coming."

Miss Melissa glared at Bernie, and I knew that Mistress Coyne saw it; wasn't no love lost between those two women, be sure of that!

"Thank *you*, Mr. Abernathy," she said. "But I must confess, I'm not sure why I am here."

Bernie blinked at that, and he and I both looked at Jamie.

"She wouldn't say a thing to me," Jamie blurted out. "So's I brought her."

"Ah," Bernie said.

Miss Melissa suggested, "Jamie, tell us what happened."

He glanced about, but there wasn't any there as didn't want him to speak, so he spoke. "Well, you sent me to talk to a man I know and ask as to who Mistress Coyne was, and I did that, and he told me as he didn't know a thing about her, save where she lived and what she looked like, and that she was at the governor's palace every so often, and that the governor was at her place on occasion, and as the two of them sent notes back and forth. And I figured as that probably wasn't all you'd wanted me to find out, so I asked for more, and he swore as how that was all he knew, but he could show me her place, and I said as I'd be pleased if he did, so he did, and there she was, and I was looking in the door—it's a little tea-room that she runs. Anyway, I was looking in the door, and she saw me and asked me what I wanted, and I didn't know as what I should say, and she asked who I was, and I told her, and she asked as who sent me, and I said that I was from the *Bonny Anne*, and she asked as whether Captain Dancy had wanted something of her, and I allowed as how I hadn't any idea, and then she asked if the ship was in port, and I said of course it was or I wouldn't be there, and next thing I knew she was coming with me back to the ship to see what was happening, and here we are."

He stopped as if the words had run out sooner than he'd expected, and had surprised him in doing it, and he sort of blinked at us in confusion.

"Thank you, lad," Bernie said. He turned to Mistress Coyne and asked, "It seems to me, mistress, that you came here of your own will, and that you know why better than we."

"I'll tell you what I know, Mr. Abernathy," she replied tartly. "I know that Captain Dancy had told me his ship would be leaving port at midnight, and here it is after that when a boy turns up at my shop saying that the *Bonny Anne* is still in port, and with a tale of being sent to find out who I am, when Jack Dancy has known me well these several months past. So I came to see what's become of the captain. I'd hoped to see him here on his own quarterdeck, and instead I find you in command. Could you tell me why?"

Bernie harrumphed—did a fine job of it, too, rocking back on his heels. "Well, mistress," he said, "As it happens, the captain is indisposed. Very much so, I'm afraid. Our ship's doctor, Emmanuel Brewer, is tending to him now."

Mistress Coyne said, in a very quiet voice, "I'm sorry to hear that."

"So were we," Bernie replied. "And after he was taken ill, we had word from Governor Lee that he was concerned over some agreement he had made with the captain. The message was not at all clear, I fear, but it did let us know that the Governor took the matter, whatever it is, very seriously. Being loyal subjects of the Crown, we wanted to do our best to carry on despite the captain's temporary inconvenience—but I'm afraid the captain had neglected to inform any of us of just what it was the Governor wanted. However, your name was mentioned in the Governor's message, so we thought perhaps you could shed a little light on the situation."

"I see," said Mistress Coyne. I looked away for a moment to judge our position—the cliffs to port loomed up black and appeared a good bit closer than I really cared to see them.

When I looked back Mistress Coyne was lifting her veil, and the light from the mizzen lantern caught her face full. I swallowed and tried not to stare.

It was plain to me in that instant why she had worn a veil; a face like that isn't to be risked parading openly through the streets of Collyport at night.

"Jack Dancy didn't tell you *anything?*" she asked.

We all shook our heads—Bernie, Miss Melissa, myself, even Jamie.

"Jamie, run along and get some sleep," I said, now that I'd recalled he was there.

The others turned to stare as Jamie started a protest, and when he met all those eyes he thought better of arguing. He shuffled away, disappointed.

"You've not mutinied, have you?" Mistress Coyne asked, once Jamie was clear.

Bernie and I were honestly shocked, but I saw as how she could think it might be. We both spoke at once, but I think we made it plain we'd done no such a thing.

Mistress Coyne looked about, and asked, "Where are we? Where are you taking me?"

Bernie started to say something about how it wasn't her concern, but I spoke up and said, "We're bound to a place we know of around the other side of the island. The captain told us that much, though we were late on gettin' a start."

"Do you know what you're to do there?"

"No."

She nodded. "I see." She studied us, and then looked Miss Melissa straight in the eye and asked, "And who might you be?"

Miss Melissa took a deep, angry breath and turned red as a boiled lobster. Bernie spoke up before she could shout, though.

"This is Mistress Melissa Dewhurst, a good friend of Captain Dancy and aboard the *Bonny Anne* at the captain's personal invitation."

"I'm delighted to meet you, Mistress Dewhurst," Mistress Coyne said with a nod, "but I fear that you must be bored by all this chatter?"

Miss Melissa drew another breath, but this time 'twas myself who stopped her.

"Miss Melissa," I said, "I'd take it as a great favor if you would go below and see whether there's been any change in the captain's condition." And I pointed to the cabin skylight.

She nodded, and gave Mistress Coyne a look such as I hope I never receive from any woman, and then marched off the quarterdeck.

Once she was gone I kept an eye on the cabin skylight, lest Miss Melissa be clumsy in opening it to hear, while Bernie asked, "Now, Mistress Coyne, if you don't mind, is there anything you can tell us?"

She looked about dubiously, and saw that the only people on the quarterdeck were herself, and Bernie, and me, and Black Eddie at the wheel. She could hardly expect the helmsman to leave his post, and Bernie and I were the captain's two senior officers and two of his closest friends. None of the men in the rigging were close to hand.

"I don't know the details of Captain Dancy's plan," she said, "but I do know what Governor Lee wants of him. He's to remove Madame Lee."

Bernie looked puzzled. "Remove Madame Lee?" he repeated.

Mistress Coyne nodded.

"Remove how?"

"Alive."

That was some relief, in any case; I'd no particular desire to kill a woman, and besides, it hardly made sense to hire a man like Jack Dancy as a mere assassin. There's many a simpler way for a man to kill his own wife, should he care to.

There'd been that fellow on Pennington's Cay, for one—but no, that wasn't all that much simpler at that, and not relevant to the present case.

I tried to recall what I'd heard of Madame Lee.

The Governor had brought her back from another island five years before, and had held a wedding that was still the subject of many a barroom tale or boast, though there wasn't but two people actually killed that day, and at least one of them clearly deserved it. I'd no idea what her maiden name might have been, or which island she'd come from, nor for that matter of much else about her. I'd never laid eyes on her, nor had any man I knew of, not to swear to. I knew precious little about her, if the truth be known.

There were rumors, of course, but I'd not put faith in rumors, after some as I'd heard where I knew the truth of the matter. Why, the rumors would have it that Jack Dancy...well, they lied, and enough of that.

But as to the discussion we were having with Mistress Coyne, the next word spoken came from Mr. Abernathy.

"Why?" Bernie asked, and in my heart I cursed the man for a fool. Hadn't he heard what Jamie had said? Hadn't he seen Mistress Coyne's face? It was as plain to me as I might want that the Governor had it in mind to keep company with Mistress Coyne, and for that sort of entertainment the presence of a previous wife can hamper one a mite.

"Why alive, do you mean?" Mistress Coyne asked, and I realized perhaps Bernie wasn't the fool I thought, as it was a sound question. As I said, there's many a simpler way for a man to kill his own wife, and in particular when the man is the governor and chief magistrate of a crown colony, and none's to argue if he says his wife fell from a cliff and wasn't pushed, or that the meal she died of was rotten but not poisoned.

But then I saw Bernie's face, and knew that he *was* a fool. He started to say, "No, I meant—" but I cut him off.

"Aye," I said, "It seems to me as that's a sound question."

"Well, because...well, there are reasons that..." She stopped, cross with herself, and started over. "I don't know for certain why the Governor wants her taken alive, but I do know something about her that might have something to do with it."

I nodded, "And what might that be?"

Mistress Coyne grimaced. She said, "Madame Lee is a witch."

5.

Hasty Bernie and I looked at each other, and we each saw the dismay in the other's eyes.

We had both battled the Black Sorcerer with Jack Dancy. We were both beside him when he fought the devil-kites at Bethmoora, and when the night thing came aboard in Dunvegan Sound. Bernie was there when he outwitted the Pundit of Oul. I was there when he sweet-talked the ship and the lives of a dozen men, myself among them, away from the Caliburn Witch. We'd both seen Doc Brewer work a few little spells, and even those could be enough to terrify any sane man. And we'd both seen enough of other magic to know that neither of us cared to see more.

The prospect of kidnapping a witch was not exactly one that cheered the either of us.

And here we were with little choice, when it came right down to bottom, but to do that very thing. In fact, we were already asail toward the caves, and I knew now why. It wasn't to meet anyone, there was no rendezvous we'd missed; it was because through the caves we could get into the Governor's Palace and catch Madame

Lee and bring her out the same way without being seen and without stumbling across the palace guards, as we might have done by any other route.

That is, unless the captain had been planning something complicated, as he might have been, but as we had no way of knowing.

I thought about it for a moment.

The warehouse fire was to get us out to sea without arousing suspicion—and so as to provide an alibi, as well, for later on, should anyone be looking into the matter of Madame Lee's disappearance, Jack Dancy could swear that he and his ship weren't even in the harbor at the time, so how could he be involved?

And Mistress Coyne and the Governor's letter fit in, as well—I judged that Mistress Coyne and Governor Lee had got a mite impatient with the impediments they'd been encountering and wanted the captain to get on with it.

After all, if Governor Lee had made his arrangements with the captain *three years ago*...

The patience of the man would fair qualify him for sainthood, if that were the truth of it, but thinking it over I saw as it wasn't likely that the whole plan had been made that long ago. Not many's the man that keeps the same mistress *and* the same wife so long as that. Besides, the governor had only been married two years at that point, which seems a tad hasty in tiring of a wife. No, my guess was that the governor's agreement with the captain was merely that at some time the governor would set the captain a task to discharge his debt, and that this was the task he'd come up with.

And a task worthy of Jack Dancy's talents it was, too, kidnapping a witch. Even *he* hadn't attempted it before.

I wished Jack Dancy were still alive to do it.

So the fire was accounted for, and the letter—but how did the freight wagon fit in? And the parrot?

Had we taken the wagon on board or left it on the dock? I couldn't for the life of me recall just at that moment, though I didn't recollect any order to bring it aboard, nor seeing it anywhere but the dock. I hoped it didn't matter, but I feared it did. Seeing as the captain had said the wagon was to be there at midnight, and as the fire was to be set near about midnight, I judged as we should already have done something with that damned wagon, either taken it aboard or done something with it back at the dock.

"Beggin' your pardon, Mistress Coyne," I asked, "but would you have any notion as to what use a freight wagon might be in this little enterprise we're attemptin'?"

She considered that for a moment, and then said, "No."

"I feared as much," I told her. "What about a parrot?"

She looked at me as if I were daft and asked, "What *about* a parrot?"

"Ah," I said. "Never you mind." It was plain that the captain hadn't told her any more than he had us, as to the exact details.

There wasn't much more to be done on deck until we reached the caves, so Bernie and I made some polite chitchat with Mistress Coyne for a moment, and then I slipped away to see just what might be happening elsewhere aboard the *Bonny Anne*.

First off, I saw as the freight wagon wasn't aboard. We'd left it sitting plain on the dock.

I looked into the fo'c'sle, to see the parrot for myself. There it was, on Peter Long's hammock, giving me the beady eye. I called to it, but it wouldn't say a word.

Next I betook myself down to the surgery, where Doc Brewer was sitting cross-legged, naked to the waist and painted like a savage, with black candles burning and a great clutter of skulls and suchlike about him.

He looked up when I came in, and his face was red and puffy, and the sweat was rolling down his chest like rainwater running down the masts. "Hello, Billy," he said.

"I'm not interruptin', am I?" I asked.

He shook his head. "No," he said, "It's of no use. I can't find a trace of him." He got to his feet and leaned against a bulkhead. "It's wearying, it is, calling like that."

I nodded, and tried to think of something sympathetic to say, but before the words came he asked me, "Where are we bound, Billy? I feel the ship moving. Did you find out what the captain was up to?"

"In a manner of speaking," I admitted. I took a moment to gather my nerve, and then I asked him, "Tell me, could you be handlin' a witch, if we took one prisoner?"

He blinked. "A witch, you say? Are we to capture a witch?"

I nodded. "That we are."

He turned and poked at a canvas bag that hung on the bulkhead. "That would explain this, I suppose."

"Would it, now?" I asked. "And what might that be?"

"Oh, the hide of a salamander, and the bones of an eel, and a variety of other things. The captain told me the day before yesterday to find what I'd need for making a geas, the strongest I knew how. I suppose he meant for me to put a geas on her not to harm us, or some such a requirement."

"And you have it all?" I asked. A thought struck me. "You wouldn't need a parrot, would you?"

"A parrot?" He stared at me. "I've no use for a parrot, not for this spell nor any other I know.

"Oh, well," I said, "I was just askin'. So, do you have what you need for this geas, then?"

"Oh, of course," he said, "Save for the hair of the victim."

"Well," I said, "I don't suppose 'twill be any great feat to cut a lock of her hair for you. How long will it take, once you've the hair?"

He pursed his lips and considered that, and I commenced to worry, as I had hoped he'd be telling me 'twould be no time at all. Instead he said, "Well, it would depend on just when I began, but four to six hours, most likely."

"Ah," said I, thinking about what it would be like trying to hold an angry witch prisoner for six hours, with no magic against her. I wondered what the captain had planned—had he gotten a hank of Madame Lee's hair, somehow, that Doc Brewer should have already had?

I thought he might, at that. I told Doc to get ready to start his spell and then I went back up on deck.

Peter Long met me there and asked, "Mr. Jones, what's to be done with that blasted parrot?"

"Hold onto it," I told him. "We'll no doubt know soon enough." Then I went on to the quarterdeck. Hasty Bernie and Annabelle Coyne were still talking.

"Mistress Coyne," I asked, "did the captain, by any chance, mention anything to you about Madame Lee's hair?"

She stared at me. "Now how did you know about that, Mr. Jones?" she asked lightly.

"About what, Mistress?" Bernie asked.

"About the hair. I fetched him a handful of hair, taken from Madame Lee's brush—I don't know why. I guessed he was planning to have a wig made for some part of his deceptions."

"And what became of that hair?" I asked.

"Oh, I haven't the faintest notion," she replied. "I gave it to Captain Dancy yesterday."

I closed my teeth hard to hold back a curse. "Mr. Abernathy," I said, "I'm going below, to take a look at the captain's condition."

"Very good, Mr. Jones," Bernie said.

The moment I stepped through the cabin door Miss Melissa demanded, "What's this about that woman's hair?" She stepped down from the stool under the skylight and glared at me.

"Doc Brewer needs it for a spell," I told her. "To put Madame Lee under a geas."

"Oh," she said.

"It's most likely somewhere in this cabin," I said.

"Do you think old Wheeler would know?" she asked.

That hadn't occurred to me to wonder, and I allowed as how it hadn't. She went and rousted the old man from his hammock, whilst I began opening cabinets and drawers.

Jack Dancy's old servant wasn't at his best just then, roused in the middle of the night, but at last we managed to explain that we were looking for a hank of a lady's hair that the captain had probably hidden somewhere. I hadn't found anything of the sort in my search—though some of the items I *had* found stirred my curiosity a tad. Whatever did the captain need with a playbill for an opera in Southampton? Or a shell carved to the shape of a herring? And where did he get some of those pictures?

Of course, I recognized a few of his souvenirs, like the tip off the narwhal's tooth, and the green pendant he'd got from Madame Kent after Cushgar Corners.

Well, wasn't none of that important just then.

"A lady's hair?" Wheeler asked, and we both nodded, and Miss Melissa shouted at him a little.

He paid her no mind; instead he crossed to a cabinet I hadn't tried yet, and reached around the side, and opened the cabinet door, and then reached in to the hinge and opened that same door again—the door was made in two layers that folded out.

And between those two layers were pinned a hundred locks of hair, each one tied in a ribbon.

And weren't none of them labeled or tagged.

6.

I stared at those damned locks of hair for a moment, and then I said words that I'd never have said in the presence of Miss Melissa had I remembered she was there. She said some of the same sort herself, though.

A thought struck me, then. Those hundred hanks were all the colors in which one might expect a lady's hair to be found, from ash to black with a bit of a side-trip out to red along the way. I've known men as would only take a blonde lassie, or a redhead, but never let it be said that Jack Dancy put any such arbitrary limits upon his interests.

"And what color, then," I asked, "would Madame Lee's hair be?"

There wasn't a soul there who could answer, so I betook myself back to the quarterdeck and put the same question to Mistress Coyne.

"Brown," she told me. "A middling brown."

And wouldn't you know that full forty of those lovelocks were of a middling brown?

Naturally, Madame Lee wasn't one of the four redheads, nor the lone ash blonde.

And then we were anchored below the caves, and I saw the night was growing old, and there wasn't more time to worry about it. If we were to spirit Madame Lee from the palace before her maids were up and about, we'd to do it right soon.

I gathered up a few things I thought might be of use, and then I stood on the quarterdeck with Bernie whilst the call went round for volunteers for a shore party, and the men began to gather on the halfdeck, and Hastings Abernathy and I eyed each other a bit, each hoping the other would speak first.

Hasty Bernie was the senior, though, so it was his place, and at last he sighed and said, "One of us must go ashore, Mr. Jones, and the other keep the ship."

"Aye, sir," said I, not letting a thing show.

"I don't see," he said, "as there's any necessity as to which of us takes which post."

"No, sir," I said. "Nor do I."

"D'you want to lead the shore party, then?"

"'Tis your decision, sir."

"Do it, then. As senior, my first responsibility is the ship. And besides..."

He didn't finish the sentence, but then I don't suppose he had to. We both knew as I was better at this sort of affair. Hasty Bernie was twice the seaman I was, and a finer hand with the sextant and chart than ever our poor dead captain could have hoped to be, but he weren't quite as fond of improvisation, nor as quick with a cutlass, as I was.

So I was glad of the duty because I thought I'd a better chance of pulling it off—but at the same time, I reckoned that chance to be pretty pissing poor, and I'd have been fair relieved if Bernie had taken it upon himself.

I went to the rail and looked over the men I'd be leading. There was Peter Long, and Black Eddie, and Ez Carter, and Goodman Richard—I'd no complaints about who was there and who wasn't, save that Doc Brewer might come in handy.

He was nowhere to be seen, though, and I decided against sending for him. Instead I made a little speech.

"All right, boys," said I, "the Captain's gone and gotten us into another one, and we'll just have to get ourselves out. I'll tell you what it's about on the way, not that I know meself."

And then we were climbing up the ropes to the cave mouth, and I was trying to think if there was anything more I should have brought, besides the lantern, and matches, and the cutlass, and the brace of pistols, and the powder and shot, and the dagger, and the sack of biscuit, and the flask of rum, and the fifty feet of line, and the cosh in my pocket.

A little gold might have been nice, in case any bribery were called for. I had three shillings in my purse, and that was all.

Well, it didn't seem worth going back for.

The caves were dark as the Dungeon Pits on Little Hengist until I got the lantern going. Then I had to remember the route without the Captain leading the way, which took me a little bit of a moment.

I managed it, though, with only the one wrong turning, and despite what he said to me between oaths I swear that Black Eddie's foot was still a good ten feet from the brink of the pit when I realized we'd have done better to have turned left than right at the big pillar.

We came out in the palace wine cellar and stopped to catch our breath and look the matter over.

"Well, now," I said. "Here we are in the palace, and ahead is the stair to the kitchens, and from there we're to find Madame Lee. Being the hour that it is, I'm thinking she'll be in her chamber. Now, where would that be?"

Black Eddie and Peter and the others stared at me like as if I'd just ordered them hanged.

"Don't you *know?*" Peter asked.

"There's no need to be takin' that tone with me, Peter Long," I told him. "No, the fact is I *don't* know. How would I? Nor would any man aboard the ship, for that matter."

"Any man, no," Good Richard pointed out, "but what about the women? Or Jamie?"

I didn't think Miss Melissa knew even as much as I did, but I saw as how he could have a point where Jamie McPhee and Mistress Coyne were considered.

"Well, it's too late now," I said. "We're here and they're not and we've to make the best of it. Be ready, but no pistols—we don't want to rouse the whole palace. Come on, then."

I drew my cutlass and led them up the stairs with the blade naked before me, and the four of them followed at my heel with their own swords out.

At the top we gathered tight together whilst I worked the latch, and then the door opened and we all tumbled out into the kitchens, blades at the ready.

There were two people there, a man and a girl, and I judged them to be the palace baker and either his assistant or a scullery girl. Ez and Peter ran up to them and had steel at their throats in a trice.

I put down my lantern, but kept my sword ready as I walked over, a bit more leisurely than Ez and Peter had. I tried to behave as if I burst into places like this an hour before dawn, taking prisoners, as a regular thing.

"Tell us truth and no harm will come to you," I said.

They said not a word, but just cowered there, mouths agape. I took it for acceptance.

"Where is Madame Lee's chamber, then, and how do we get there from here?" I demanded.

The baker, if such he was, looked at me with even greater astonishment, but the scullery girl piped up, "It's in the north wing. You cross the hall to the stairs, go up two flights, and around, and then down the corridor to the right, and it's the last door on the right."

A fine girl, that—would blab anything to anyone. "Thank you, lass," I said, and then I looked the situation over and felt some misdoubt about it.

If we left these two free, they might raise the alarm. If we bound them, they might be found—and besides, I thought we might need all the rope we had for other uses.

"Eddie," I said, "You stay here and watch these two, and make sure neither of them tells a soul we're about."

Eddie opened his mouth to say something, most probably to protest being asked this, but then he took another look at the girl and changed his mind. "Aye aye, Billy," he said.

"Good, then. You others, come along, and try to be quiet about it."

With that, I led them along the course the lass had described.

We crossed the hall and found the stairs, climbed the stairs and found the corridor, and then we stopped, for the wench hadn't mentioned that a guard was posted outside the door of Madame Lee's chamber.

And what was worse, he saw us before we saw him.

I was wavering there between giving it all up as a botch and fleeing back down the stairs, or charging ahead, since we did outnumber him four to one and perhaps if we were quick we could convince him not to rouse the palace, when he called in a loud whisper, "*There* you are! My Lord, you're two hours late!"

I blinked at him, and then grinned, and I led the lads down the passage. I saw Ez Carter sheathe his sword, but the rest of us kept ours ready.

"Hurry up," the guard hissed, "My relief is due soon, and nobody bribed *him*."

We scurried up to the door beside him, and none of us had said a word yet.

"What kept you?" he asked me. "And where's your captain?"

"The Captain had a bit of a mishap," I said. "A whack on the head. He's in his bunk aboard ship."

"Is he all right, then?"

"Oh, as right as he'll ever be," said I, which was true after a fashion.

He nodded, and then he took a glance at a window at the end of the corridor, which I had not until that moment noticed. "The wagon's ready?" he asked.

"Um," said I, and I heard Ez Carter swearing under his breath.

The guard insisted, "Is the wagon below the window there, ready to catch her?"

"Well, no," I admitted. "If the truth be known, it's not. We had a little mishap—the same one as hit the captain on the head, do you see."

At the least, I thought, now I knew what the wagon had been intended for.

The sentry looked disconcerted, as if he'd just seen a tax collector smile, but before he could say anything more the bedchamber door opened and a woman's head thrust out, long hair hanging free, not decently put up.

"What're the lot of you doing here whispering outside my door at this hour?" she said.

Good was the first of us to react. He dropped his sword and grabbed for her, and caught her round the neck with one arm and pulled her out into the hallway. She was a tall wench, and thin, with hair the color of mahogany, and I thought me I knew the face from somewhere. She wore a black nightdress trimmed with lace, a pretty thing, and clearly not meant to be seen in public. When Good Richard laid hold of her her arms flew up to either side, and she made a noise like a spitting cat.

And Goodman Richard shriveled down away from her, and was turned into a toad, right before our eyes.

Whilst the rest of us were still staring, Ez Carter caught her across the back of her head with a belaying pin he'd had in his belt, and witch or no witch, she went down in a heap.

"That's her?" I asked the guard.

He nodded, staring.

I had me a thought, wagon or no wagon. I took a quick few steps to the window at the end of the passageway and looked out.

I could see all of Collyport from there, spread out before me, and the harbor beyond. The warehouse fire had died down some, but still glowed orange. All the same, I could see that some of the ships had put back into port; the *Armistead Castle* was back at her berth, but I couldn't put names to the others.

I looked down, then, to where a wagon might have waited, if we'd have had one.

Sure enough, there was a road down there—but it was a hundred feet down, and the wall was sheer stone.

The captain might have planned to take Madame Lee out that way, but I wasn't about to try it. I'd brought rope, but not enough, and I hadn't brought any tackle to secure it. Nor did I know where the road went, and men on foot, carrying a woman, would be slower and more likely to attract notice than a freight wagon would have been.

We'd have to go back out the way we came—for one thing, aside from the rest, we'd left Black Eddie in the kitchen. I turned back.

"Come on, then, this way," I called to the others, snatching up the toad and tucking it in my pocket with one hand while my other retrieved Good's cutlass. "Pick her up between you and come along!"

"Wait!" the guard called, "You can't...You owe me five guineas for this!" With a start, I remembered Captain Dancy's last words. I also remembered the three shillings in my pocket and frowned. "And besides," the man continued, "when they find me..."

Ez Carter gave me a look, and I nodded. He let go his side of the woman, and while Peter Long hoisted her up across his shoulder, Ez walked up and whacked the guard soundly across the pate with his belaying pin.

He sat down suddenly against the wall, and a moment later, when I glanced back from the corner, I saw him reach up to rub his head. I could see the lump from there.

We none of us worried about him; with an eye on the witch, who was already beginning to stir, we ran for the kitchens.

Black Eddie was waiting, with the baker and the maid. The baker had his hands tied behind him and was perched on a stool, facing a wall; the wench wasn't tied at all.

"Come on," I told Eddie, and he buttoned his pants and came on. The girl got to her feet and looked around, and at the sight of Madame Lee her eyes widened.

"Maybe we'd best bring her along," Eddie suggested.

"Please yourself," I told him, not caring to waste time arguing, "As long as she doesn't slow us down."

He grabbed her wrist, and Ez grabbed the lantern, and we all trampled down the stairs to the wine cellars, Ez first, then Peter with Madame Lee over his shoulder, then me, and then Black Eddie, dragging his girl along by her wrist.

I saw as how leaving the baker as we had meant that the secret route through the caves would be a secret no more, but I didn't see any way that could be helped, since we'd no wagon outside the window to escape in, as the captain's plan had called for, and I'd no stomach for killing the baker in cold blood. A corpse in the kitchen might well tell the tale in any case.

Madame Lee raised her head from Peter's shoulder and looked at me, and I began to wonder what flies tasted like.

"Madame," I called, with my best manner, "before you act rashly, remember there are four of us left, and if you enchant another, the rest will kill you in self-defense." I lifted the cutlass that was still in my hand. "We mean you no harm, I promise."

I was none too certain that cold steel would kill a witch as easily as that, but I hoped.

And I was more certain than ever that I knew that face, though with the long hair flying loose about it, and all of us bouncing giddily down the stairs, I couldn't place it just then.

We reached the bottom and ran through the cellars, through the door into the caves, where we found ourselves in gloom relieved by only the single lantern—it seemed worse, somehow, than it had on the way in. I looked, and saw the glass was a trifle smoked, as the wick needed trimming. I wished I'd brought more than the one, as we'd no way to trim the wick there.

Well, a man can't think of everything, and we had the one, and it was still enough to see by. I tucked the cutlass in my belt—I had two there now, my own and Goodman Richard's. "This way," I said.

"Mr. Jones," Peter said, "might I put her down for a moment? Or could someone else carry her?"

"Is she heavy?" Ez asked.

"Not so you'd notice," Peter said, "But it's awkward, carrying a woman about that way, all on one side."

"I can walk," Madame Lee said, and she raised her head again, and when I saw her face in the lantern-light and heard that throaty voice again I recognized her at last.

"Oh, my good Lord in heaven, and all the saints and angels," I said, staring. "It's the Caliburn Witch herself."

7.

She blinked at me, and then smiled like a cat stretches. "Billy Jones," she said. "You've a few more gray hairs than when last we met, haven't you?"

"By God I do," I agreed. "And you're the cause of a few of them!"

She just smiled at me again as Peter set her on her feet.

"You've sworn not to harm us," I told her, "For as long as Jack Dancy lives, you're sworn not to touch a single man of the *Bonny Anne*'s crew."

"Well do I know it," she answered, still smiling. "And where *is* Captain Dancy?"

"Aboard ship," I said. "He's feeling poorly."

The smile winked out like a blown candle-flame.

"My Jack?" she said. "My Jack's ill?"

"I'll say no more," I told her. "It's not my place."

The other men were staring. Ez and Peter hadn't yet joined the crew six years before, when we'd tangled with the Witch; Eddie hadn't gotten a good look at her face in the dash down the cellar stairs, and hadn't been in the passageway when she came out of her room. And poor Good, of course, was a toad—I could feel him squirming about in my pocket—so he couldn't have said anything if he recognized her.

They'd all heard of the Caliburn Witch, though. Everyone in the islands had heard of the Caliburn Witch. Sometimes we'd wondered why none had heard anything *new* of her these past few years.

In a way, though, dangerous as she was, I was glad to see her there, for she *had* sworn not to harm us, and wouldn't likely flee at the first chance. We might not need Doc Brewer's geas at all.

And of course, against the likes of her, the best geas Emmanuel Brewer could concoct might not be any more use than trying to bail the ocean dry with my hat. The Caliburn Witch was not to be held lightly.

It occurred to me that Captain Dancy hadn't known which witch he'd been sent after, or he'd not have bothered about a geas. That was something that might bear a little more thought when I had time.

Just then, though, the toad in my pocket was still squirming, and that squirm reminded me. I pulled Good out of my pocket and held him out. "Can you change him back now, if you please? You *did* swear not to harm him."

She smiled that cat-smile again. "Surely I swore that, but I don't see that he's been harmed. He looks a fine, fat, healthy toad to me."

I frowned at her. "I'd reckon it harm to turn a man to a toad, and I think so would the captain. He's lost the use of his voice, hasn't he? Don't you reckon that as harm?"

She shrugged. "It might be said so," she admitted. "Alas, I can't turn him back here and now. I keep a spell ready to hand at night, against just such as you, but I'd never any need before for the cure, and I haven't got it with me."

I was about to argue, when Eddie said, "Billy, shouldn't we be getting back to the ship?" He pointed at the lantern, which was burning low and smoking more than ever.

I looked, and saw that he had a sound argument. "Come on, then," I said, tucking the toad away, and we wound our way back through the caverns to the sea.

I feared we might have to tie the witch up and lower her down hand over hand, but she gave us no trouble about scampering down the lines, as if climbing ropes were something she did every day between the Governor's audiences.

Then again, for all I knew she might have been able to fly down, but she didn't.

The kitchen wench rode down pickaback on Black Eddie, arms about his neck and legs about his waist, and he damn near lost his hold a time or two on account of the added weight.

At the last, though, we were all down safely and back aboard the *Bonny Anne*, and the moment I came up the side, bringing up the rear as befit my position in command of the party, Hasty Bernie gave the order to up anchor and take us back to Collyport.

He was safe up on the quarterdeck, seeing to the ship, and the rest of my party was scattering to their posts in the rigging, whilst I found myself on the halfdeck with the four females.

"Which one is Madame Lee?" Miss Melissa asked, puzzled, though how she could think a lass as young as that serving maid could be the Governor's wife of five years I don't know. Governor Lee had his faults, but I'd never heard any say pedophilia was one of them.

"Who's that?" Mistress Coyne demanded, jabbing her thumb at Eddie's wench.

"Mistress Coyne!" the girl said, staring at the Governor's woman, "What are *you* doing here?"

"Who are t*hese* two?" asked the Caliburn Witch suspiciously.

I sighed, and tried to decide where to begin.

A croak from my pocket decided me.

"Madame Lee," I said, "Allow me to present Mistress Melissa Dewhurst, who's aboard the *Bonny Anne* at Captain Dancy's personal invitation."

The two women glared at one another, but before either could speak I turned to the next. "And Mistress Annabelle Coyne," I said, "who came aboard to assist us in certain matters, and who had the misfortune to be caught on board when a fire on the docks compelled us to depart."

She smiled graciously at Madame Lee, though with a little more tooth showing than might be strictly necessary.

"And I'm afraid," I said, "That I didn't catch the name of the young lady who came aboard with Black Eddie."

"Susan Bowditch," said the wench, and she dropped a curtsy.

"Mistress Bowditch," I said with a bow. "Welcome aboard. And you, too, Madame Lee, of course."

Madame Lee paid me no heed. She was staring at Mistress Coyne with that cat-smile on her face again. I'd never seen it until an hour or so before, but already I was growing sore weary of that expression.

"I begin," she said, "to understand. Rouse Jack Dancy out here, I've something to tell him."

I exchanged a glance with Miss Melissa.

"I'll see if he's to be roused," Miss Melissa said, and she turned away and trotted to the cabin.

The ship was heeling over as we rounded the Seal Stones, and I could see Mistress Coyne shifting as she tried to keep her balance. Poor little Susan Bowditch had to grab for the rail, and I guessed she'd be seasick soon.

The Witch, of course, didn't notice. It would take more than a ship's motion to bother *her*.

"Ladies," I began, thinking we might go below, and then I stopped.

I couldn't take them down to the cabin, not with the captain's corpse still stretched out there. The wardroom that I shared with Bernie was hardly a fit place for them, the fo'c'sle even worse. The black, airless depths of the hold would hardly be an improvement.

The gundeck, perhaps?

I decided we'd do best to stay where we were.

I looked about. The sky was lightening in the east; Bernie had a good lot of canvas spread, and we were making way nicely. I judged we'd be back in Collyport within an hour, if the wind didn't turn foul.

An hour on deck in such mild weather would do no harm.

"Excuse me for a moment, ladies," said I, and I trotted over to the starboard shrouds, where Black Eddie had just descended to the deck.

"Eddie," I said, "What were you thinking of, bringing the wench along?"

"I'm sorry, Billy," he said. "She just got the better of me for a moment."

"Will it trouble you any if we put her ashore when we make port?" I asked.

He thought about that for a moment. "She's a pretty little thing," he said, "But I suppose it'd be best."

That was one problem solved—and as I watched Mistress Bowditch lurch against the rail and spew over the side I didn't doubt that she'd want to be put off the ship.

I knew what the wagon had been for, now—that was another problem solved. The captain had meant for us to come in through the caves, but go out through the window, so that the route in would remain a secret, safe for later use. He'd probably have told the baker that we crept in earlier and hid in the wine cellars.

And we'd done what the Governor wanted—another problem gone.

Now there were just three more that I saw left to us.

First, now that we had the Witch aboard, what were we to *do* with her?

Second, how were we to keep her from discovering that Jack Dancy was dead, and that her oath not to harm us was thereby void? She'd sworn long ago that the Bonny Anne and all aboard would be hers when Jack Dancy died.

And third, what was the parrot for?

Well, I judged that solutions would either present themselves or not, and in the meanwhile there were things to be done.

I glanced over, and saw Mistress Coyne and Madame Lee exchanging words, and with them looks meant to freeze the heart. Little Susan Bowditch was still sick at the rail.

And here came Miss Melissa back again.

"My apologies, Madame Lee," she said, "But the captain's in no state to be seen, nor will he be for some time yet."

The Witch gave a smile worse than any I'd yet seen on her face, and I thought my heart would stop.

"Mistress Dewhurst," she said, "I've seen Jack Dancy at his worst."

Miss Melissa threw me a puzzled and angry look, and I told her, "Madame Lee once held the captain prisoner for a fortnight, six years ago."

The Witch grinned. Jack Dancy had been her prisoner, right enough—but not in the dungeons with the rest of us.

I could see that Miss Melissa didn't know what to make of that, but she could hardly ask for explanations just then. "All the same," she said, facing up to the witch with a courage I didn't know she had, "Aboard his own ship, he'll not be seen at his worst."

I tried to distract them all by saying, "Mistress Coyne, we'll be back in port shortly, and we'll be sending you ashore there."

She was about to reply when a cry came from the masthead, "Sail ho!"

We all looked up, and I called, "Where away?"

"Dead ahead!" came the reply.

We looked, and sure enough, there was a frigate rounding the point ahead, just where we'd been headed. We were closing on her quickly, and she was turning broadside to, rather than continuing on her course. She was scarce a quarter mile away—the headlands had hidden her—and we were bearing down on her.

"What colors?" Hasty Bernie called from the quarterdeck.

"She's flying the Governor's flag," came the reply. "She's the *Armistead Castle!*"

That was all right, then— we all knew the *Armistead Castle*. We'd seen her in port that night, seen her ahead of us when we put out to sea, and I'd seen her back at her moorings from the palace window. She was the Governor's own ship that he called out to chase away any pirates foolish enough to venture into Collyport without his permission, and as we were on the Governor's business, so to speak, we'd naught to fear from her.

We were just beginning to relax when she opened fire.

8.

It wasn't a full broadside, just a warning shot, but the ball whistled overhead and scared the bloody hell out of us all.

"What the hell?" I asked, and that was the mildest remark I heard on that deck. Miss Melissa and Mistress Coyne said far worse; Madame Lee and Mistress Bowditch didn't bother with words.

"Heave to!" Bernie called, and the men hurried to obey, while the women and I stood there amidships, all of them talking at once, trying to figure out what was happening.

"Hail her," Bernie ordered the man at the masthead, but the lookout called down, "They're lowering a boat!"

That meant a parley, I judged.

I began to have an idea what was happening. I couldn't be sure, though, and I thought I'd best cover every possibility I could. I pulled the rope from my waist, that line I'd taken into the caves and not used.

"Your pardon, ladies," I said, and I proceeded to bind their hands behind them—first Madame Lee, and then Mistress Coyne, and just to be sure I went on and tied Mistress Bowditch and Miss Melissa, as well.

Miss Melissa started to protest, but I whispered, "Bear with me, Mistress, please."

She shrugged and let me tie her hands.

Then I drew one of the two cutlasses on my belt and waited for the parley boat to arrive.

A few minutes later—which seemed like half of eternity—the boat bumped up against the side. A couple of the men secured it, and Peter Long, who was one of them, called, "Officer coming aboard, Mr. Jones!"

As the officer's cocked hat appeared in the entry port I lifted the sword to Madame Lee's throat.

The man's face was shocked, when he saw me standing there behind a row of women, all with their hands bound, and one with my blade against her neck.

"My Lord, man," he began, and then stopped.

"Speak your piece," I told him. "Why'd you fire on us?"

He blinked, and then said, "I'm here at the Governor's orders, sir. He'd heard that the crew of the *Bonny Anne* had abducted an innocent woman from Collyport, one Mistress Annabelle Coyne, and he came down to the port and sent us out after you."

I blinked back at him, much relieved. The Governor hadn't double-crossed us, then, and wasn't going to sink us for kidnapping his wife. Instead, he'd thought we were double-crossing *him*, and stealing the wrong woman.

"Governor Lee's aboard your ship?" I asked.

"Yes, sir, he is," the officer replied.

"Well, then, you can tell him he's been misinformed. Mistress Coyne was not kidnapped; she came aboard of her own free will, and she's free to go, any time she chooses." I turned the cutlass about and used it to cut the cords on Mistress Coyne's wrists. Then I cut Mistress Bowditch's, as well—this was as good a time as any to get her out of the way. I pushed them both toward the officer. "Here she is," I said, "And another as well, and you're welcome to take them back with you."

The officer stammered for a moment, and then asked Mistress Bowditch, "You're Annabelle Coyne?"

"No," Mistress Coyne said angrily, "I am."

Mistress Bowditch was still too seasick to say anything; she just nodded.

"And those other two?" the Governor's man asked, pointing.

"Spoils of war," I said, "and none of your concern."

I thought that the Witch would betray me, and I think for a moment she thought so, too, but instead she grinned.

"They don't speak English," I added.

The Witch nodded eagerly. Miss Melissa glowered at me, but kept silent.

The officer—a lieutenant, he was, by his uniform—looked about, and then decided to take what he was given and see what happened. "This way, ladies," he said, and he helped Mistress Coyne and Mistress Bowditch down over the side.

Then the boat pulled away, and Miss Melissa shouted, "Get these ropes off me!"

Madame Lee didn't say a word, but the ropes fell away from her wrists.

I set to untying Miss Melissa, and spoke up cheerfully. "There, now, ladies, we've settled that! We're rid of those two, who would have been nothing but trouble, and we still have you. I take it from your silence, Ma'am, that you had no particular wish to be sent aboard the *Armistead Castle*?"

I looked at Madame Lee, and she looked back.

"Mr. Jones," she said, "I've known for some time that my husband was tired of my company, and I've no more love for him. I enjoyed playing the Governor's lady and being mistress of Collyport, but it's not worth the grief if he's going to such extremes as this to get rid of me!"

My mouth fell open.

She sneered—a harsh word to use of a lady, but she did. "Come now," she said, "Did you think I didn't know, when I saw Annabelle Coyne on this deck, that it was George Lee who had sent you to kidnap me? And furthermore, do you think I didn't know why? He's trying to rid himself of two problems at once—Jack

Dancy and myself. Jack didn't know who I was, but my dear Georgie did. So he sent you to capture me, and Jack agreed, thinking he could handle an ordinary witch—Doc Brewer's surely prepared a little spell of some sort! But then Jack was to find himself with no mere hedgerow enchantress, but the infamous Caliburn Witch aboard, the same who he had scarcely escaped six years ago. Georgie knew I'd rather stay aboard the *Bonny Anne* with my Jack than in his palace with him, and he was right!"

"*Your* Jack!" Miss Melissa burst out.

"Aye," the witch told her, "*my* Jack, or he was once, at any rate, and long before he was *your* lover. But what's it matter now, that he's dead?"

My mouth fell open, and Miss Melissa's snapped shut.

"Dead?" she said.

"How did you know?" I asked—for I knew better than to lie any more to the Caliburn Witch.

She gave me a bitter smile. "I know my Jack," she said. "If there was still breath in his body, he'd have come on deck when someone fired on his *Bonny Anne*."

We could scarce argue with that, for it was the plain truth.

"How did it happen?" the Witch asked.

"He slipped and hit his head," I said. "In the alley behind Old Joe's Tavern."

Her eyes widened. "Is that all? It wasn't the Black Sorcerer? Nor Bartholomew Sanchez? Nor the Pundit of Oul?"

"No," I said. "Just a fall and a broken neck."

She shook her head.

It was at that moment that the frigate fired a full broadside at us.

The roar swept over us, and the balls tore through the rigging; I heard lines snap and canvas tear and shot howl through the air. We all spun in astonishment.

"Man the guns!" Hasty Bernie cried from the quarterdeck, and men swarmed to the gundeck.

"*What?*" the Witch cried. "He *dares?*"

"Dares what?" I shouted back over the pounding feet and the rattling of the gun tackles, "Who?"

"That worm who called me his wife! That little bitch from the kitchens told him I was aboard, and now he means to sink us!"

"How do you..." I started to ask, but then I remembered who I spoke to. Instead I asked, "Why didn't he just sail away?"

"And let everyone aboard his ship know he was leaving his lady in Jack Dancy's hands? He couldn't do that. How could he ever hold his head up again if he sailed away and left his own wife in the hands of an adventurer like Jack Dancy?"

"But then why didn't he send a boat to parley..." I began.

"You bloody *fool!*" she shrieked, turning on me, just as the frigate's second broadside thundered out at us, "He doesn't want me back, he wants me *dead!* Even a witch can drown in twenty fathoms of salt water!"

I heard the crunch of a ball hitting the side, and saw a fore mainsail sheet flying free where a shot had snapped it, and then our own guns roared out, raggedly. Doc Brewer tottered up from below, the canvas bag of unused arcana in his fist, looking about wildly.

I knew we had no chance; the *Bonny Anne* carried eighteen guns to the frigate's thirty-two, and smaller guns at that. We had scarce thirty seamen aboard, what with having left port so hurriedly, while he surely had two hundred. "Strike!" I called to Bernie. "He can't sink us if we strike! Better a dungeon than drowning!"

"*NO!*" shrieked the Witch. She staggered across the deck and snatched the bag from Doc Brewer, then tore it open.

She looked up at me with a grin of triumph on her face, and snatched out something long and thin and yellowish. She lifted it above her head, stretched between her two hands, and shouted out something.

What she shouted was in no language I had ever heard before, nor any I ever wish to hear again.

The frigate's third broadside roared out, but when I looked at the Governor's ship I saw that it had heeled back, and that most of the balls would pass over us, too high to do any damage.

And our own ship was heeling back, as well, and the sea between us seemed to be rising up, and I tried to guess what trick of the tide or the gunfire could cause that, and then I realized it wasn't any natural trick at all.

The wave rose up higher and higher, above the level of our decks, and then still higher, above the spars; the frigate was hidden from sight now behind a rising wall of surging green water.

The Witch was standing, arms raised and spread, like a statue; wind whipped her hair about her as if she stood in a hurricane, but elsewhere the air was almost dead calm now, the sails hanging limp. Her eyes blazed with a green fire.

The water rose up until it seemed to cover half the sky—and then it fell.

On the frigate.

The backwash sent the *Bonny Anne* rocking and bouncing, yawing wildly, and I grabbed for the rail, and saw others doing the same—everyone but the Witch herself grabbed for a handhold somewhere.

Spray burst up over the side and caught me in the face.

When I was able to clear my eyes and look again, there was no trace of the *Armistead Castle* anywhere, only the rocks and the tossing waves.

The sea calmed gradually, and I heard Bernie sending the men to repair the damage we'd taken in the battle. I didn't concern myself with that; instead I paid attention only to the Caliburn Witch.

The light had faded from her eyes, and she lowered the yellowish thing and tossed it to Doc Brewer. I finally got a decent look at it, and saw that it was the skeleton of an eel.

"*That* should teach the man not to mistreat his wife!" the Witch snapped. She turned. "Mr. Abernathy!" she called. "Set a course for Drummond Isle; we'll be putting Mistress Dewhurst ashore there, in her home town!"

Miss Melissa started when she heard that, and glanced at the Witch, but didn't say anything.

"Aye aye," Bernie called back, in a puzzled tone.

I was just as puzzled. "Your pardon, ma'am," I ventured, "but what is it you're planning?"

I remembered well how, six years before, she had sworn to see me and my mates dead.

So did she, I judged.

Was she planning to set Miss Melissa ashore first, and then sink us, or burn us?

Such scruples hardly seemed likely, given that she'd had no hesitation in sending Mistress Coyne and Mistress Bowditch to the bottom, along with everyone else aboard the *Armistead Castle*. True, Mistress Coyne had been her husband's mistress, and Mistress Bowditch had tattled to the Governor, but Miss Melissa was her dead lover's woman, so she'd grounds for a grudge there, too.

"Well, Mr. Jones," she said, turning back to me with the least-malicious smile I'd yet seen on her face, "I've had my fill of the Governor's Palace, and for that matter all of Collyport. I'd seen all I cared to of Caliburn Island five years ago, or I'd not have left it. I think the time has come to roam a little, to wander about—and it seems to me that a ship and crew have just fallen into my hands that would suit me fine for that wandering. There's the little matter of your deaths, yours and a dozen others, a sentence I handed down back on Caliburn six years ago. Well, I'm willing to commute that sentence to a few years of penal servitude—aboard this ship, under my command." She made the smile into another of her cat-grins. "Or I could hang you. It's your choice, Mr. Jones."

It took me no time to decide *that* one. "Aye aye, Captain Lee," I replied, saluting.

We put Melissa Dewhurst and five crewmen who asked ashore on Drummond Isle eleven days later, where for all I know they're all living peacefully to this day. John Hastings Abernathy, who after all had never angered the Witch and hadn't been with us those six years before, was retired three months after, and put ashore in Collyport, where he took a post with the new Acting Governor as portmaster. I was promoted to first mate.

Captain Dancy we gave a fine burial at sea the very afternoon after the sinking of the *Armistead Castle*. Captain Lee turned the toad back into Goodman Richard, using Doc Brewer's paraphernalia, that same night.

As for the rest, Captain Lee says she'll set us free when she grows bored. She's no worse a master than was Jack Dancy, for the most part, and as she's taken a fancy to me I've no need now to wait until we're in port to find a woman to share my bunk.

Like most of Captain Dancy's plans, the whole affair had all worked out well enough, if not the way we expected.

I see how it was meant to work—the fire for a distraction, the entry through the caves, the escape in the wagon below the window, the geas to hold the witch under control until we could put her ashore somewhere. Captain Dancy hadn't planned to have Mistress Coyne aboard, nor to have the Governor think that Mistress Coyne had chosen Jack Dancy over himself and come out to get her back. He hadn't known that Madame Lee was no ordinary witch, but the Caliburn Witch.

It's pretty much all clear now.

But we never did find out what the damn parrot was for.

What the Parrot Was For

On the next page is the answer to a question left unanswered at the end of "The Final Folly of Captain Dancy" and you really don't want to know until after you've read the story.

(It's trivial, anyway, just a very minor detail. You'll be disappointed. I hadn't intended to answer it, but people keep asking me, so eventually I figured I might as well tell them what they wanted to know.)

So if you must know, then turn the page...

The parrot used to belong to a brothel, and will, on cue, say, "Come on boys! This way!" Captain Dancy was going to send it in a nearby window, then cue it to talk, so as to lure away the kitchen staff in the Governor's Palace. This would mean that the secret of the entrance through the wine-cellars wouldn't be given away.

So now you know.

Windwagon Smith and the Martians

I reckon most folks have heard of Thomas Smith, the little sailor from Massachusetts who turned up in Westport, Missouri one day in 1853 aboard the contraption he called a windwagon. He'd rigged himself a deck and a sail and a tiller on top of a wagon, and just about tried to make a prairie schooner into a *real* schooner. Figured on building himself a whole fleet and getting rich, shipping folks and freight to Santa Fe or wherever they might have a mind to go.

Well, as you might have heard, he got some of the folks in Westport to buy stock in his firm, and he built himself a bigger, better windwagon from the ground up, with a mainmast and a mizzen both, and he took his investors out for a test run—and they every one of them got seasick, and scared as the devil at how fast the confounded thing ran, and they all jumped ship and wouldn't have more to do with it. Smith allowed as how the steering might not be completely smooth yet, though the idea was sound, but the folks in Westport just weren't interested.

And last anyone heard, old Windwagon Smith was sailing west across the prairie, looking for braver souls.

That's the last anyone's heard till now, anyways. A good many folks have wondered whatever became of Windwagon Smith, myself amongst them, and I'm pleased to be able to tell the story.

And if you ask how I come to know it, well, I heard it from Smith himself, but that's another story entirely.

Here's the way of it. Back in '53, Smith headed west out of Westport feeling pretty ornery and displeased; he reckoned that the fine men of Westport had just missed the chance of a lifetime, and all over a touch of the collywobbles and a bit of wind. Wasn't any doubt in his mind but he could find braver men somewheres, who would back his company and put all those mule-drawn freight-wagons right out of business. It was just a matter of finding the right people.

So he sailed on, and he stopped now and then and told folks his ideas, and he was plumb disconcerted to learn that there wasn't a town he tried that wanted any part of his windwagon.

He missed a lot of towns, too, because the fact was that the steering *was* a mite difficult, and he didn't so much stay on the trail as try to keep somewhere in its general vicinity. He stopped a few times to tinker with it, but the plain truth is that he never did get it right, not so as one man could work it and steer small. After all, the clippers he'd learned on didn't steer just with a tiller, but with the sails as well—tacking and so forth. If Smith had had more men on board, to help work the sails, he might could have managed some fine navigation, instead of just aim-and-hope.

After a time, though, he had got most of the way to Santa Fe, but had lost the trail again, and he was sailing out across the desert pretty sure that he was a good long way from where he had intended to be, when he noticed that the sand was getting to be awfully red.

The sky was getting darker, too, but there wasn't a cloud anywhere in it, and it wasn't but early afternoon; it just seemed as if the sun had shrunk up some, and the sky had dimmed down from a regular bright blue to a color more like the North Atlantic on a winter morning. The air felt damn near as cold as the North Atlantic, too, and that didn't seem right for daytime in the desert. What's more, Smith suddenly felt sort of light, as if the wind might just blow him right off his own deck, even though it didn't seem to be blowing any harder than before. And he was having a little trouble breathing, like as if he'd got himself up on top of a mountain.

And the sand was *awfully* red, about the color of a boiled lobster.

Well, old Windwagon Smith had read up on the West before he ever left Massachusetts, and he'd never heard of anything like this. He didn't like it a bit, and he took a reef in the sails and slowed down, trying to figure it.

The sand stayed red, and the sky stayed dark, and the air stayed thin and he still felt altogether too damn light on his feet, and he commenced to be seriously worried and furled the sails right up, so that that windwagon of his rolled to a stop in the middle of that red desert.

He threw out the anchor to keep him where he was, and had a time doing it, because although the anchor seemed a fair piece lighter than he remembered, it almost took him with it when he heaved it over. Seemed like he had to be extra careful about everything he did, because even the way his own body moved didn't seem quite right; of course, being a sailor, he could keep his feet just about anywhere, so he got by. He might have thought he was dreaming if he hadn't been the level-headed sort he was, and proud of his plain sense to know whether he was awake or asleep.

Just to be sure, though, he pinched himself a few times, and the red marks that left pretty much convinced him he was awake.

He stood on the deck and looked about, and all he saw was that red, red sand, stretching clear to the horizon whichever way he cared to look. The horizon looked a shade close in, at that; wasn't anything quite what it ought to be.

He didn't like that a bit. He climbed up aloft, to the crow's nest up above the main topsail, and he looked about again.

This time, when he looked to what he reckoned was west, he saw something moving, something that was blue against the blue of the sky, so he couldn't make out just what it was.

It was coming his way, though, so he figured he'd just let it come, and take a closer look when he could.

But he wasn't about to let it come on him unprepared. After all, there were still plenty of wild Indians around, and white men who were just as wild without any of the excuses the Indians had, seeing as how they hadn't had their land stolen, or their women either, nor their hunting ruined. They could be just as wild as Indians, all the same.

He slid down the forestay and went below, and when he mounted back to the maintop he had a sixgun on his belt and a rifle in his hand.

By now the blue thing was closer, and he got a good clear look at it, and he damn near dropped his rifle, because it was a ship, a sand ship, and it was sailing over the desert right toward him.

And what's more, there were three more right behind it, all of them tall and graceful, with blue sails the color of that dark sky. Proud as he was of his work, old Windwagon had to admit that the ugliest of the four was a damn sight better-looking than his own windwagon had ever been, even before it got all dusty and banged up with use.

They were quieter, too. Fact is, they were near as silent as clouds, where his own windwagon had always rattled and clattered like any other wagon, and creaked and groaned like a ship, as well. All in all, it made a hell of a racket, but these four sand ships didn't make a sound—at least, not that Smith could hear yet, over the wind in the rigging.

He was pretty upset, seeing those four sand ships out there. Here he'd thought he had the only sailing wagon ever built, and then these four come over the horizon—not just one, but four, and any of them enough to burst a clipper captain's heart with envy.

If they were freighters, Smith knew that he wasn't going to get anywhere near as rich as he had figured, up against competition like that. He began to wonder if maybe the folks back in Westport weren't right, but for all the wrong reasons.

The sand ships' hulls were emerald green, and the trim was polished brass or bone white, and above the blue sails they flew pennants, gold and blue and red and green pennants, and they were just about the prettiest thing Smith had ever seen in his life.

He looked at them, and he didn't know what the hell they were doing there or where they'd come from, but they didn't look like anything wild Indians would ride, or anything outlaws would ride, so he just watched as they came sailing up to his own ship—or wagon, or whatever you care to name it.

Three of the sand ships slowed up and stopped a good ways off, but the first one in line came right up next to him.

That one was the biggest and the prettiest, and the only one flying gold pennants. He figured it must belong to the boss of the bunch, the commodore or whatsoever he might be called.

"Ahoy!" Smith shouted.

He could see people on the deck of the sand ship, three of them, but he couldn't make out any faces, and none of them answered his hail. They were dressed in robes, which made him wonder if maybe they weren't Indians after all, or Mexicans.

"Ahoy!" he called again.

"Mr. Smith," one of them called back, almost like he was singing. "Come down where we can speak more easily."

Smith thought about that, and noticed that none of them had any guns that he could see, and decided to risk it. He climbed down, with his rifle, and he came over to the rail, where he could have reached out and touched the sand ship if he stretched a little.

He was already there when he realized that the strangers had called him by his right name.

Before he could think that over, the stranger who had called him said, "Mr. Smith, we have brought you here because we admire your machine."

Smith looked at the strangers, and at the great soaring masts and dark blue sails, and at the shiny brass and the sleek green hull, and he didn't believe a word of it. Anyone who had a ship like that one had no reason to admire his windwagon. He'd been mighty proud of it until a few minutes ago, but he could see now that it wasn't much by comparison.

Well, he figured, the strangers were being polite. He appreciated that. "Thanks," he said. "That's a sweet ship you have there, yourself."

While he was saying that, he noticed that the reason he hadn't been able to make out faces was that the strangers were all wearing masks, shiny masks that looked like pure silver, with lips that looked like rubies. The eyes that showed through were yellow, almost like cat's eyes, and Smith wasn't any too happy about seeing that. The masks looked like something Indians might wear, but he'd never heard of any Indians like these.

He said, "By the way, I'd be mighty obliged if you could tell me where I am; I lost my bearings some time back, and it seems as if I might be a bit off course."

He couldn't see which of the strangers it was that spoke, what with the masks, but one of them said, "My apologies, Mr. Smith. It was we who brought you here. You are on Mars."

"Mars?" Smith asked. He wasn't sure just how to take this. "You mean Mars, Pennsylvania? Down the road apiece from Zelienople?" He didn't see any way he could have wound up there, and he'd never heard tell that Pennsylvania had any flat red deserts, but that was one of the two places he'd ever heard of called Mars, and he didn't care to think about the other one much.

"No," the stranger said. "The planet Mars. We transported your excellent craft here by means that I am unable to explain, so that I might offer you a challenge."

Now, Smith knew something about the planets, because any sailor does if he takes an interest in navigation, and he knew that Mars was sort of reddish, and the red sand would account for that nicely. He looked up at that shrunken sun and that dark blue sky, and then at those sand ships like nothing on Earth, and decided that one of three things had happened.

Either he'd gone completely mad without noticing it, and was imagining all this, which didn't bear thinking about but which surely fit the facts best of all; or somebody was playing one hell of a practical joke on him, which he didn't have any idea how it was being done; or the stranger was telling the truth. For the sake of argument, he decided he'd figure on that last one, because the second seemed plumb unlikely and the first wasn't anything he could figure on, never having been mad before and not knowing just how it might work. Besides, he'd simply never judged himself for the sort of fellow that might go mad, and he wasn't in any hurry to change his mind on that account.

So he figured the stranger was telling the truth. Whether it was magic, or some sort of scientific trick, he didn't know, but he reckoned he really was on Mars.

And he didn't figure he'd ever find his way back to Earth by himself.

"What sort of a challenge?" he asked.

He sort of thought he saw the middle stranger smile behind his silver mask.

"I," the middle stranger said, "am Moohay Nillay, and I am the champion yachtsman of all Teer, as we call our planet." Smith wasn't any too sure of those names, so I may have them wrong. "I have the finest sand ship ever built, and in it I have raced every challenger that my world provided, and I have defeated them all. Yet it was not enough; I grew bored, and desired a new challenge, and sought elsewhere for competitors who could race against me."

Smith began to see where this was leading, but he just smiled and said, "Is that so?"

"Indeed it is, Mr. Smith. Unfortunately, our two worlds are the only two in this system bearing intelligent life, and your world has not produced many craft that will sail on sand. I am not interested in sailing upon water—our planet no longer has any seas, and I find the canals too limiting. I might perhaps find better sport on the seas of your planet, but the means by which I drew you here will not send me to Earth. I have been forced to wait, to search endlessly for someone on your planet who would see the obvious value of sailing the plains. To date, you are only the second I have discovered. The first was a man by the name of Shard, Captain Shard of the *Desperate Lark*, who fitted his sea-going ship with wheels in order to elude pursuit; I drew him here, and easily defeated his clumsy contrivance. I hope that you, Mr. Smith, will provide a greater test."

"Well, I hope I will, Mr. Nillay. I'd be glad to race you." Smith didn't really think he had much of a chance against those sleek ships, but he figured that it wouldn't hurt to try, and that if he were a good loser, Mr. Nillay might send him back to Earth.

And of course, there was always the chance that his horse sense and Yankee ingenuity might just give him a chance against this smooth-talking Martian braggart.

Well, to make a long story a trifle less tiresome, Smith and the Martian agreed on the ground rules for their little competition. They would race due south, to the edge of a canal—Smith took the Martian's word for just where this canal was, since of course he didn't know a damn thing about Martian geography. Whoever got there first, and dropped a pebble into the canal without setting foot on the ground, would win the race.

The Martian figured it at about a two-day race, if the wind held up, and he gave Smith a pebble to use—except it wasn't so much your everyday pebble as it was a blue jewel of some kind. Smith hadn't ever seen one quite like it.

If Smith won, he was to have a big celebration in the Martian's home town, and would then be sent back to Earth, if he wanted. If he lost, well, he wouldn't get the celebration, but if he had put up enough of a fight, made it a good race and not a rout, the Martian allowed as he might consider maybe sending him back to Earth eventually, just out of the goodness of his heart and as a kind gesture.

Smith didn't like the sound of that, but then he didn't have a whole hell of a lot of choice.

"What about those other folks?" he asked, figuring he needed every advantage he could get. "I'm sailing single-handed, and you've got two crewmen and three other ships."

The Martian allowed as how that might be unfair. Captain Shard had had a full crew for his ship, and Mr. Nillay hadn't been sure whether Smith had anyone else aboard or not, but since he didn't, since he was sailing alone, then Mr. Nillay would sail alone, too. And the other three ships were observers, just there to watch, and to help out if there was trouble.

Smith couldn't much quarrel with that, so after a little more arguing out details, the two ships were lined up at the starting line, Smith's windwagon on the left and the Martian sand ship on the right, both pointed due south.

One of the other Martians fired a starting pistol that didn't bang, it buzzed like a mad hornet, and the race was on.

Old Windwagon yanked the anchor aboard and started hauling his sheets, piling on every stitch of canvas his two little masts could carry, running back and forth like a lunatic trying to do it all by himself as fast as a full crew, all the while still keeping an eye on his course and making sure he was still headed due south.

Those sails caught the wind, and before he knew it he was rolling south at about the best speed he'd ever laid on, with nothing left to do but stand by the tiller and hope a crosswind didn't tip him right over.

When he was rolling smooth, he glanced back at the Martian sand ship, and it wasn't there. He turned to the stern quarter, and then the beam, and he still didn't see it, but when he looked forward again there it was, a point or two off his starboard bow, that tall blue sail drawing well, full and taut, and that damn Martian yachtsman standing calm as a statue at the tiller.

And although it wasn't easy over the rattling and creaking of his own ship, Smith could hear the Martian sand ship make a weird whistling as it cut through that red sand.

Well, seeing and hearing that made Smith mad. He wasn't about to let some bossy little foreigner in a mask and a nightshirt beat him *that* easily, no sir! He tied down the tiller and ducked below, and began heaving overboard anything he thought he could spare, to lighten the load and help his speed.

Extra spars and sails, his second-best anchor, and the trunk with his clothes went over the after rail; he figured that he could come back and pick them up later if he needed them. When the trunk had hit the ground and burst open, he turned and looked for that Martian prig, and was about as pleased as you can imagine to see that he was closing the gap, gaining steadily on the Martian ship.

Then he hit a bump and went veering off to port, and had to take the tiller again.

Well, the race went on, and on, and Smith gained on the Martian little by little, what seemed like just a few inches every hour, until not long after sunset, while the sky was still pink in the west, the two ships were neck and neck, dead even.

It was about at this point that it first sank in that they weren't going to heave to for the night, and Smith began to do some pretty serious worrying about what might happen if he hit a rock in the dark or somesuch disaster as that. He hadn't sailed his windwagon by night before.

He wasn't too worried about missing a night's sleep, as he'd had occasion to do that before, when he was crewing a clipper through a storm in the South Pacific, or spending his money ashore in some all-night port, but he *was* worried about cruising ahead under full sail across uncharted desert in the dark.

It helped some when the moons rose, two little ones instead of a big one like ours, but he still spent most of that night in a cold sweat. About his only consolation was that the crazy Martian was near as likely to wreck as he was himself.

It was a mighty cold night, too, and he wrapped himself in all three of the coats he still had and wished he hadn't been so quick to throw his trunk over.

About the time when he was beginning to wonder if maybe the nights on Mars lasted for six months, the way he'd heard tell they did way up north, the sun came up again, and he got a good look at just where he stood.

He'd pulled ahead of the Martian, a good cable's length, maybe more. He smiled through his frozen beard at that; if he just held on, he knew he'd have the race won.

So he *did* hold on, as best he could, but something had changed. The wind had died down some, and maybe the Martian had trimmed his sails a bit better, or the wind had shifted a trifle, but by the middle of the afternoon Windwagon saw that he wasn't gaining any more, and in fact he might just be starting to lose his lead. He wasn't the least bit pleased, let me tell you.

He started thinking about what else he had that he could throw overboard, and he was still puzzling over that when he topped a low rise and got a look at what lay ahead.

He was at the top of the longest damn slope he'd ever seen in his life, a slope that looked pretty near as big as an ocean, and down at the bottom was a big band of green, and in the middle of that green was a strip of blue that Smith knew had to be the canal.

And it was downhill almost the entire way!

The green part wasn't downhill, he could see that, but that long, long red slope was. It wasn't steep, and it wasn't any too smooth, but it was all downhill, and that meant he didn't want to lighten the ship any more at all.

He tied down the tiller again and hung down over the side, pouring on the last of his axle grease so as to make the most out of that hill.

When he got back up on deck and looked back he could see that he was gaining quickly now, pulling farther and farther ahead of the Martian's lighter ship. And that canal was in sight, straight ahead! He figured he just about had it won.

And then the wind, which had been just sort of puffing for awhile, up and died completely.

By this time he was rolling hell-for-leather down that hill, at a speed he didn't even care to guess, and he didn't stop when the wind died—but that flat stretch of green ahead suddenly looked a hell of a lot wider than it had before.

He pulled up the tiller entirely, to cut the drag; after all, the canal stretched from one horizon to the other, so what did he need to steer for? He could still maneuver the sails if he had to.

He went bouncing and rattling down that hill, thumping and bumping over the loose rocks and the red sand, praying the whole way that he wouldn't tip over. He didn't dare look back to see where the Martian was.

And then he was off the foot of the slope, crunching his way across that green, which was all some sort of viney plant, and his wagon went slower, and slower, and slower, and finally, with one big bounce and a bang, it came to a dead stop—a hundred feet or so from the canal.

Smith looked down at those vines, and then ahead at that blue water, and then back at the Martian sand ship, which wasn't much more than a dark spot on the red horizon behind him, and he just about felt like crying. There wasn't hardly a breath of wind, just the slightest bit of air, enough to flap the sails but not to fill them.

And what's more, the vines under his wheels weren't anywhere near as smooth as the red sand, or the prairie grass back on Earth, and he knew it would take a good hard tug to get the old windwagon started again.

If he could once get it started, he figured that he could just about reach the canal on momentum, without hardly any wind; the vines sort of petered out in about another twenty feet, and from there to the canal the whole way was stone pavement, smooth white stone that wouldn't give his wheels the slightest bit of trouble.

But he needed a good hard push to get off those vines and get moving, and the wind didn't seem to be picking up, and that Martian was still sailing, smooth and graceful, closer and closer down the slope.

And thinking back, Smith recalled that the sand ship had a blade on the front. He hadn't seen much use for it back on the sand, but he could see how it would just cut right through those vines.

He looked about, and saw that a dozen or so Martians, in their robes and masks, were standing nearby, watching silently. Smith wasn't any too eager to let them see him lose. If there was ever a time when he needed some of that old Yankee ingenuity he prided himself on, Smith figured this was it.

He looked down at the vines again, and thought to himself that they looked a good bit like seaweed, back on Earth. He was stuck in the weeds, just like he might be on a sandbar or in shoal water back on Earth.

Well, he knew ways of getting off sandbars. He couldn't figure on any tide to lift him off here, but there were other ways.

He could kedge off. He hauled up the anchor, and heaved it forward hard as he could—and the way his muscles worked on Mars, that was mighty hard. That anchor landed on the edge of the pavement, and then slid off as he hauled on it, and bit into the soft ground under the vines.

That was about as far as he could haul by hand, though. For one man to move that big a wagon, even on Mars, he needed something more than his own muscle. He took the line around the capstan and began heaving on the pawls.

The line tautened up, and the wagon shifted, and then inched forward—but he couldn't get up any sort of momentum, and he couldn't pull it closer than ten feet from the pavement, where it stopped again, still caught in the vines. When he threw himself on the next pawl the anchor tore free.

He hauled it back on board and reconsidered. Kedging wasn't going to work, that was pretty plain; he couldn't get the anchor to bite on that white stone. So he was still on his sandbar.

He thought back, and back, and tried to remember every trick he'd ever heard for getting a ship off a bar, or freeing a keel caught in the mud.

There was one trick that the men o' war used; they'd fire off a full broadside, and often as not the recoil would pull the ship free.

The problem with that, though, was that he didn't have a broadside to fire. His whole armory was a rifle, two sixguns, and a couple of knives.

He looked back up the slope, and he could see the sand ship's green hull now, and almost thought he could see the sun glinting on Mr. Nillay's silly mask, and he decided that he was damn well going to *make* himself a broadside—or if not a broadside, at least a cannon or two.

The wind picked up a trifle just then, and the sails bellied out a bit, and that gave him hope.

He went below and began rummaging through everything he had, and found himself his heavy iron coffeepot. He took that up on deck, and then broke open every cartridge he had and dumped the charges into the pot; he judged he had better than a pound of powder when he was through. He took his lightest coat, which wasn't really more than a bit of a linsey jacket anyway, and folded that up and stuffed it in on top of the powder for a wad. He put a can of beans on top for shot, and then rolled up a stock certificate from the Westport and Santa Fe Overland Navigation Company and rammed it down the coffeepot's spout for a fuse.

The sails were filling again, but the wagon wasn't moving. Smith figured he still needed that little push. He wedged his contraption under the tiller mounting, and touched a match to the paper.

It seemed to take forever to burn down, but finally it went off with a roar like a bee-stung grizzly bear, and that can of beans shot out spinning and burst on the hillside, spraying burnt beans and tin all over the red sand. The coffeepot itself was blown to black flinders.

And the wagon, with a creak, rolled forward onto the pavement. The sails caught the wind, feeble as it was, and with rattling and banging the windwagon clattered across that white stone pavement, toward the canal.

And then it stopped with a bump, about ten feet from the edge, just as the wind died again.

Smith just about jumped up and down and tore at his hair at that. He leaned over the rail and saw that there was a sort of ridge in the pavement, and that his front wheels were smack up against it. He judged it would take near onto a hurricane to get him past that.

He looked back at the Martian sand ship, with its long, graceful bowsprit that would stick out over the canal if it stopped where he was, and he began swearing a blue streak.

He was at the damn canal, after all, and the Martian was just now into the vines, and he wasn't about to be beat like that. He knew that he had to *drop* the pebble, not throw it, so he couldn't just run to the bow and heave it out into the water. He was pretty sure that that old Martian would call it a foul, and rightly, if he threw the confounded thing.

And then that old horse sense came through again, and he ran up the rigging to the mainyard, where he grabbed hold of the starboard topsail sheet and untied it, so that it swung free. Hanging onto the bottom end, he climbed back to the mizzenmast, up to the crosstrees, still holding the maintopsail sheet, and dove off, hollering, with the pebble-jewel in his hand.

He swooped down across the deck, lifting his feet to clear it, and then swung out past the bow, up over the canal, and at the top of his swing he let the pebble drop.

It plopped neatly into the water, a foot or two out from the canal wall, while that Martian yachtsman was still fifty feet back. Windwagon Smith let out a shriek of delight as he swung wildly back and forth from the yardarm, and a half-dozen Martians applauded politely.

By the time Smith got himself back down on the deck, Mr. Nillay had got his own ship stopped on the pavement, and he was standing by the edge of the canal, and even with his mask on Smith thought he looked pretty peeved, but there wasn't much he could do.

And then a few minutes later the whole welcoming committee arrived, and they took Smith back to their city, which looked like it was all made out of cut glass and scrimshaw, and they made a big howdy-do over him, and told him he was the new champion sailor of all Mars, the first new champion in nigh onto a hundred years, and they gave him food and drink and held a proper celebration, and poor old Mr. Nillay had to go along and watch it all.

Smith enjoyed it well enough, and he had a good old time for awhile, but when things quieted down somewhat he went over to Mr. Nillay and stuck out his hand and said, "No hard feelings?"

"No, Mr. Smith," the Martian said, "No hard feelings. However, I feel there is something I must tell you."

Smith didn't like the sound of that. "And what might that be, sir?" he asked.

"Mr. Smith, I have lied to you. I cannot send you back to Earth."

"But you said..." Smith began, ready to work himself up into a proper conniption.

"I did not believe I would lose," the Martian interrupted, and his voice still sounded like music, but now it was like a funeral march. "Surely, a sportsman like yourself can understand that."

Well, Smith had to allow as how he *could* understand that, though he couldn't rightly approve. It seemed to him that it was mighty callous to go fetching someone off his home planet like that, when a body couldn't even send him back later.

Old Nillay had to admit that he had been callous, all right, and he damn near groveled, he was so apologetic about it.

But Smith had always been philosophical about these things. It wasn't like he'd had a home anywhere on Earth; all he'd had was his windwagon, and he still had that. And there on Mars he was a hero, and a respected man, where on Earth he hadn't been much more than a crackpot inventor or a common seaman. And the food and drink was good, and the Martian girls were right pretty when they took their masks off, even if they weren't exactly what you'd call white, being more of a brown color, and those big yellow eyes could be mighty attractive. What's more, what with Martians being able to read minds, which they could, that being how they could speak English to Smith, the women could always tell just what a man needed to make him happy, and folks were just generally pretty obliging.

So Windwagon Smith stayed on Mars and lived there happily enough, and he raced his windwagon a few more times, and mostly won, and all this is why he never did turn up in Santa Fe and why he never did find any more investors after that bunch in Westport backed out.

And I know you may be thinking, well, if he stayed on Mars, then how in tarnation did I ever hear this story from him so as I could tell it to you the way I just did, and all that I can say is what I said before.

That's another story entirely.

One Million Lightbulbs

John Chester Glatfelter stared at the newspaper in astonishment. "Is this right?" he demanded. "It's not a typesetting error?"

Charlie Beckett, Glatfelter's personal secretary, glanced over Glatfelter's shoulder to see where his employer was pointing.

"One million electric lights," he read aloud, "illuminate the splendors of Dreamland."

"One *million*? They can't really mean that."

"I think they do, sir," Beckett murmured. "I've heard the figure before."

"Twenty years ago there weren't a million light bulbs in the entire city of New York! Now they've got that many in this one silly playland?"

"So it seems, Mr. Glatfelter."

"How can they afford it?"

Beckett shrugged—not obviously, more to himself than to his employer. "I understand that Mr. Reynolds raised a considerable sum of money for the construction of Dreamland," he said. "I believe it was more than three millions of dollars."

"Reynolds?" Glatfelter turned to glare at his secretary. "*Bill* Reynolds? Is that scoundrel behind this?"

Beckett pointed to the fine print at the bottom of the newspaper advertisement. "Mr. William H. Reynolds," he said.

"If that don't beat all," Glatfelter said, squinting at the tiny type. "What's Bill Reynolds doing, messing around with playgrounds out the hind end of Brooklyn?"

"Well, sir," Beckett explained, "Mr. Tilyou's Steeplechase Park has been such a success that it's inspired others. Last year it was those two showmen, Thompson and Dundy, with their so-called Luna Park—they spent a million dollars and used two hundred and fifty thousand electric lights. So this year Mr. Reynolds has gone them one better, and opened Dreamland, for more than *three* million dollars, and with a hundred thousand lights on the central tower alone, a million in all." He hesitated, then added, "It's quite a spectacle, sir."

Glatfelter turned again. "You've been there?"

Beckett cleared his throat. "Yes, sir. I've taken my girl Polly out there three or four times now."

"I'll be damned," Glatfelter muttered. "A sensible fellow like you, wasting your nickels on Coney Island?"

"Yes, sir. It's really quite enjoyable."

"Amazing." He stared at the newspaper for a long moment, then announced, "Beckett, if they're even getting people like *you* out there, then there's money to be made—and I'll be damned if I'm going to let that fool Reynolds make it all, while I'm left out!"

"Noisy," Glatfelter said. He looked around critically. "Is this the best place you could find?"

"Yes, sir," Beckett said, nodding, and trying not to stare at the stranger Glatfelter had brought along. "You'll understand, most of the owners on Coney Island aren't interested in selling; they find it quite profitable. This is the only location where I could put together a decent parcel of land."

"Well, it'll have to do, then. Not the best spot, but when we're done it'll look like a glimpse of heaven." He frowned. "We can dig a channel to the sea there," he said, pointing, "and put our lagoon just there, with the tower behind it."

"Ah... you're planning a lagoon and tower, sir?"

Glatfelter turned and glared at him.

"Beckett," he said, "does Luna Park have a lagoon?"

"Yes, sir."

"Does it have a tower?"

"Yes, sir."

"Does it make pots of money?"

"Yes, sir."

"And does Dreamland have a tower?"

"Yes, sir."

"And does Dreamland make pots of money?"

Beckett hesitated, and Glatfelter continued without waiting for an answer. "Of *course* we'll have a lagoon, and a tower, and everything the other parks have, and we'll make it all bigger and better! That scalawag Reynolds probably thought he'd topped Luna Park so completely he'd put it right out of business, with his million lightbulbs, but he ain't seen nothing yet, my boy! Dr. Petworthy and I will show *him* a thing or two!"

"Dr. Petworthy?"

Glatfelter gestured at his silent companion, a cadaverous man wearing a worn black frock coat and a flamboyant black mustache. "*This*," Glatfelter explained, "is Dr. Emil Petworthy, the world's foremost expert in the physiology of fun!"

Beckett blinked.

"Good heavens, boy, you didn't think I'd come out here blind, did you?" Glatfelter shouted. "I'm planning to invest ten millions of dollars in Miracle Park—I'm not going to just throw that away!"

"Well, no..."

"So I went to the University—to Columbia—and I asked 'em who was the top man in the science of enjoyment, whatever the hell they called it, and they talked for awhile, and then they sent me to Dr. Petworthy, here, the world's top authority on phallicology..."

"Felixology," Petworthy corrected, in a nasal squeak.

"Whatever."

"I see," Beckett said. He stared in dismay at the self-proclaimed felixologist, with the horrible suspicion that the faculty at Columbia had played a cruel joke on his employer firmly embedded in his mind.

"Dr. Petworthy," Glatfelter explained, "has determined that it's the electrical machinery that makes these parks so much fun for the lower classes."

"What?" Beckett's stare shifted briefly to his employer, then back to Petworthy.

"Yes," Petworthy explained, "it's the electrical fields. They affect the brain, you see. All those electric lights create what I call a euphorogenic field—they create a feeling of lightness, a pleasurable sensation. Naturally, the more refined and trained senses of the educated classes are less susceptible, but the working classes obviously enjoy it very much indeed."

"Right," Glatfelter said. "It makes 'em happy. So we'll put our tower right *there*, with a million lightbulbs on it, and Dr. Petworthy will wire it up to make the biggest, strongest you-forget- it field in history..."

"Euphorogenic."

"Whatever. Those others, Tilyou and Thompson and Reynolds, they did it by accident, whatever they may think; they still don't know that these electrical fields are the *real* reason their customers are so happy. *We* will do it on purpose, we'll give the customers a taste of paradise, and as for those others, we'll run 'em all into bankruptcy court!" Glatfelter chuckled.

Petworthy grinned, a hideous, skeletal grin.

Beckett licked his lips nervously and didn't say a word.

✦

"You don't need all that stuff," the electrician said, pointing at the tangle of brown-cloth-wrapped wire, the chunky solenoids, the oddly-wound coils.

"I know," Beckett said. "But follow the plans."

"It's a waste," the electrician insisted. "That dope Petworthy, he don't know anything about wiring. Thinks he's Dr. Tesla or somebody."

"I know," Beckett repeated. "But Mr. Glatfelter wants it done just the way Dr. Petworthy says."

"It's gonna pull current like nobody's business," the electrician warned.

Beckett rubbed his head, which was starting to ache. "Just do it, will you?"

"Putting a million lights on this tower—you know, the way it is now, when the micks come to America and sail into the harbor, first thing they see is the light from Coney Island. Mr. Beckett, I swear, when you get this thing working they'll be able to see it without leaving Ireland. Mr. Edison's gonna be rolling in dough. You'll need a half-dozen men working full-time just to replace the ones that burn out."

"Just do it and shut up," Beckett said.

The electrician shrugged. "You're the boss," he said, turning away.

✦

"But Mr. Glatfelter," Beckett said, "you *can't* open with the place like this!" He waved one arm in a sweeping gesture that took in the half-finished cyclorama of "Moses in Sinai," the "Palaces of Babylon" scenic railway that had yet to make a run without a car jumping the track, the workmen repainting the facade on the House of A Thousand Delights for the fifth time.

"Sure we can," Glatfelter said. "The season's starting. We don't want to miss Memorial Day."

"But Miracle Park is *not finished!*" Beckett insisted. "The customers will be disappointed."

"No, they won't," Glatfelter gloated. "Dr. Petworthy says the tower's all ready to go."

"But the *rides* aren't, the *exhibits*—you've had everyone working on that tower and the lagoon, and..."

"That tower's all we need to make Miracle Park the biggest money-maker in America!"

"Mr. Glatfelter, nobody's going to pay money just to see a million lightbulbs!"

"They'll pay their dimes to feel good, boy, for something that'll take them away from their worries for a little while, and that's what Petworthy's machine will do for them!"

"Have you *tested* it? What if Dr. Petworthy's theories don't work?"

"Of course they work!"

"Have you *tested* it?"

Glatfelter glared angrily at his subordinate. "No, we haven't tested it," he said, "because how *can* we test it, without a crowd of customers?"

"You could see how it looks," Beckett suggested desperately. "The sun's setting, you could see how it looks. You could see how it affects the workmen."

Glatfelter rubbed his chin, considering that. He threw a glance sideways at the tower—a replica of the Leaning Tower of Pisa, built somewhat larger than the original, painted every color of the rainbow, and with a steeper slant that Petworthy claimed would enhance the effects of the euphorogenic field. Every visible surface was covered with lightbulbs, and Beckett knew that the interior was jammed full of wiring and machinery, most of which, the electricians all agreed, would do nothing except draw current and maybe overheat.

In fact, three electricians had walked off the job, claiming the thing wasn't safe, and the fire marshal had needed a bribe almost three times the going rate.

"Sure," Glatfelter said. "Turn it on and let's see how it looks." He grinned. "It'll look like a little bit of heaven, Beckett—all that light, those colors—you'll see."

Beckett smiled with relief. He was sure that Miracle Park could work, could make money—but as a legitimate amusement park, not because of Petworthy's crackpot theories or crazy machinery. Probably the best thing that could happen would be if the tower burned itself down right now.

"Joe," he called, "turn on the tower lights, would you?"

The foreman, who had been lounging a few paces behind the big shots, looked up. He turned and looked at the tower, leaning out over the lagoon, bristling with clear glass spheres and brightly-painted arches.

"Not my job, Mr. Beckett," he said nervously.

Beckett's smile vanished. "Do it anyway. Or you won't have *any* job."

Joe sighed, and headed for the switch-house by the main gate.

A moment later, he called back, "Here she goes!"

A low whine sounded, and with a sudden blaze of incandescent brilliance, one million lightbulbs flared into life; light and color exploded across the lagoon and courtyard of the unfinished Miracle Park.

Everyone blinked, closing their eyes against the sudden glare. Hands flew up to shield eyes, and the men squinted.

"Bright," Beckett said. It seemed, in fact, much brighter than even a million lightbulbs ought to be.

"We just weren't expecting it," Glatfelter said, but for the first time in the four years since he had met Mr. Glatfelter, Charlie Beckett heard a tinge of doubt in the millionaire's voice.

Something popped, and hot glass sprinkled on the flagstones as a lightbulb exploded. The whine rose slightly in pitch. Cautiously, Beckett turned to look at the tower through the slit between his fingers.

Bands of color seemed to be moving up and down the diagonal cylinder, and the overall glow was pulsing rhythmically.

"Mr. Glatfelter..." Beckett began.

The whine suddenly soared madly upward in both pitch and volume, becoming an ear-splitting scream; instinctively, Beckett closed his eyes and turned away.

The sound went up into the ultrasonic, where it could not be heard, only felt as a painful pressure in the ear; more lightbulbs burst, and a fine spray of glass particles spewed out across the lagoon. The tower shimmered.

And no one saw what happened next; everyone there, from J.C. Glatfelter down to the merest workman in Miracle Park, had turned away from that unbearable brilliance. All they saw, through closed eyelids and shielding hands, was a sudden dimming.

And the pressure in their ears was gone; the sound had stopped.

Slowly, cautiously, Charlie Beckett uncovered his eyes and turned to look.

The tower was gone, and in its place...

He didn't really have words for it. It was like a bubble, or maybe a hole. It wasn't really there at all, in a way, and what he saw was not what had replaced the tower, but what he could see of what lay beyond it.

And what lay beyond it was a street—not one of the rowdy, cluttered streets of Coney Island, or any of the crowded streets of 1905 New York, but a gleaming black band between towering buildings that shone pink in the light of the setting sun. Women in strange tight clothing walked on one side of the street, and a glittering red machine drifted down the center. Flying things that were not birds sparkled far overhead.

And then it vanished, with a pop like another lightbulb exploding, and the lagoon and courtyard were back, dim and pale in the gathering gloom of early evening.

"How'd it look?" Joe called from the door of the switch-house. "I know you didn't say, but the switch was getting hot and sparking, so I figured I'd better turn it off... Hey!"

Glatfelter stared at the empty foundation beside the lagoon where a moment before his tower had stood, and then slowly turned to face Joe.

"Where'd the tower go?" Joe asked.

Glatfelter glowered for a moment; then he turned to Dr. Petworthy.

"All right, Petworthy," he said, "where *did* my tower go?"

Petworthy just shook his head and continued staring.

Beckett cleared his throat.

"Mr. Glatfelter," he asked, "did you see it, before Joe turned it off?"

"I saw it," Glatfelter admitted. "I don't know what the heck it was, but yes, I saw it."

Beckett's mouth twisted wryly.

"Well, Mr. Glatfelter," he said, "you *said* that tower would show folks a glimpse of heaven..."

Glatfelter threw Beckett a startled glance. "*That?*" he said. "Ha! A glimpse of heaven? Some damn fool electrical mirage, like those nickelodeon shows." His eyes narrowed. "But you just might have something, at that. Petworthy, if Joe hadn't shut the electricity off, would we still be able to see whatever it was?"

"I don't know," Petworthy said, staring at the empty foundation.

"Well, why not?" Glatfelter demanded. "Wasn't that your you-forget-it field at work?"

No one bothered correcting Glatfelter's mispronunciation this time. Petworthy slowly shook his head. "No, sir," he said, "I don't know *what* that was."

"Well, whatever it was, I want you to build me another one, and this time we won't let it disappear on us!"

"Sir..." Petworthy struggled to get the words out. "Mr. Glatfelter...I can't."

"Why not?"

"Mr. Glatfelter—I made it up as I went along, to impress you. I thought the million electric lights would create the euphorogenic field all by themselves; the rest was just for show, so it wouldn't look too easy."

For a moment Glatfelter was utterly speechless, rising up on his toes and dropping back, rising up and dropping, blowing air out through his mustache. Beckett fought down laughter.

"Well, then," Glatfelter said at last, "you can make it up as you go along *again*, damn it, and you can do it until you get it right. And when you've got it right, we'll open Miracle Park." He rose up on his toes again, and a smile began to spread beneath his whiskers. "And we'll have an attraction like nothing else," he said. "We'll show them all how it's done, we will—we'll make George Tilyou look like an amateur, Thompson and Dundy like dabblers, Reynolds and his flunky Gumpertz like fools. A glimpse of heaven!" He grinned. "One million lightbulbs, illuminating a glimpse of heaven!"

✢

Throughout the 1906 summer season Miracle Park stood closed and dark while workmen rebuilt the tower, and only incidentally continued work on the other rides and exhibits. Steeplechase Park and Luna Park and Dreamland took in millions of dollars, while Miracle Park earned not a single cent on Glatfelter's seven million dollar investment.

In 1907 Elmer Dundy died, and his long-time partner, Frederic Thompson, began to lose interest in Luna Park. Thompson's drinking problem worsened, but Luna continued to earn money.

That same year Steeplechase Park burned to the ground; George C. Tilyou, undaunted, charged a dime admission to the smoldering ruins and immediately began rebuilding. The new Steeplechase was bigger and better, but still, in its way, just as tacky—and more profitable than ever.

Miracle Park did not open; Dr. Petworthy spent the entire year experimenting with the wiring in the tower, but all that happened was that the lightbulbs blazed brightly while the coils and solenoids soaked up incredible quantities of electricity without doing anything. The rest of the park was complete, but J.C. Glatfelter wanted his tower and its vision of Heaven, or the future, or Mars, or whatever it was.

"Miracle Park could make money without it," Beckett pointed out one afternoon, as Glatfelter glared up at the brightly-painted tower. "Steeplechase never had any towers."

"The hell with the money," Glatfelter replied. "I want it to work!"

✛

By 1908 attendance had dropped off at Dreamland, the spectacular wonderland with its million lightbulbs. In fact, Glatfelter's investigators reported that it was losing money steadily.

"How do you explain that?" Glatfelter demanded, shaking the report under Petworthy's nose. "Your euphemisms aren't working!"

Petworthy frowned, then glanced up at the tower; a tangle of bare wire was woven through the upper tiers now. "It's not the lights that do it, after all," he said. "My earlier theory wasn't complete. It's something about the metal. It's that steel racetrack around Steeplechase that keeps it popular."

Glatfelter stared for a moment; Petworthy wandered off, back toward his tower, looking rather dazed.

Glatfelter let him go, then turned to Beckett. "You," he said. "I want you to go to Steeplechase, and Luna, and I want you to find out what makes them so much fun."

"Dr. Petworthy says it's the metal," Beckett pointed out mildly.

"Dr. Petworthy is a complete loon," Glatfelter snapped. "What does he know about fun? But he knows electricity, and he made that tower thing work once, so maybe he can do it again. And meanwhile, I want *you* to learn about fun."

"Well, I don't know, it isn't part of my job and I don't see how I could do it alone..."

Glatfelter snorted. "I know what you're doing, boy. State your terms, then."

The haggling didn't last long. Glatfelter paid Charlie Beckett and his girl Polly five dollars a day to explore Steeplechase and Luna, trying to figure out what made them fun.

✦

Dr. Emil Petworthy disappeared mysteriously from his laboratory in 1909, and his whereabouts thereafter remain a mystery to this day. John C. Glatfelter, convinced that Dr. Petworthy had somehow once again opened an electrical gateway to another world, spent the rest of his life and his fortune hiring electrical experimenters in unsuccessful attempts to duplicate the feat.

Charlie and Polly Beckett tried for three years to convince Glatfelter to open Miracle Park, but eventually gave up. With the money they had saved and the knowledge of what makes people laugh that they had acquired at Coney they moved to Los Angeles, where they made a fortune in the movies.

✦

In 1911 Dreamland burned to the ground, putting an end to Coney Island's spectacular era. No one ever seriously considered rebuilding; the manager, Samuel Gumpertz, instead opened a freak show on the site. Where Dreamland once stood is now the New York Aquarium.

Luna Park closed in 1946; Steeplechase went in 1964.

Miracle Park, John Chester Glatfelter's stupendous experiment in euphorogenics, never opened; the unfinished buildings eventually weathered away, and today an apartment complex stands on the site.

My Mother and I Go Shopping

My mother always knew all the best places to shop, all the tricks and bargains. You could send her out with ten dollars and she'd come home with stuff you swore would cost a hundred or more. When I was a kid I was slow learning how money worked because it seemed as if my mother could stretch it as far as needed, no matter how little there was; as a result, I had trouble with concepts like 'broke' and 'unaffordable.'

I never knew how she did it; I thought shopping was dull, and I never went along.

She did it, though. After I grew up and went off on my own, she kept on in the old home town, bringing home bargains and somehow living on my Dad's pension. I got married, and divorced, and married, and divorced, and she kept on at the old homestead.

I stopped in sometimes when I could, but she didn't seem to need me around, so I didn't make it a regular thing. It wasn't as if we'd been all that close, as these things go.

But Mother was getting on, she'd been on the far side of eighty for a couple of years, and she couldn't get around as well any more. Her eyesight wasn't good enough to drive, and she'd lost her license. Usually her friends would take care of her, but the day inevitably came when no one else was around, and she needed to pick up a few items, and I was nearby, back in the area on business.

So my mother and I went out shopping—and I must admit, despite years of listening to her and even following her around as a kid, I'd never quite figured out how she found the bargains she did, so I didn't really mind a chance to see her in action again. I assumed it would mostly be boring beyond belief, but I thought I might learn something.

I did.

The first thing I learned was that my mother still wasn't taking any sass from her youngest, even if I was forty years old.

"Do you want to go to the mall, Mother?" I asked, as I helped her into the car. "It's a nice place..."

She snorted. "It's a den of thieves," she snapped. "You just go where I tell you."

"Yes'm," I said; I kept the sigh in until I'd closed the car door.

I got in the driver's seat and asked, "Where to, then?"

"You just drive," she said, making brushing gestures at me. "I'll tell you where to go."

So I drove.

We headed in toward town, and I thought we were headed for the big old department stores downtown, maybe for the bargain basements, but then Mother snapped, "Turn right at the corner."

I turned right, onto a street I vaguely remembered but couldn't name.

"Left," she said, and we turned into the potholed alley behind a row of shops, and then right onto old brick pavement, and right again, and we were on muddy gravel between two smoke-blackened brick walls, and I'd lost my bearings completely. I was pretty sure that wherever we were, I'd never been here before.

It didn't look like a very good neighborhood, either, and I was a bit worried—Mother had been coming here to shop? Where was there to shop here, anyway? Warehouses, maybe? All I could see was brick walls, boarded windows, and padlocked doors.

Maybe it was just a shortcut.

Then we turned another corner, and another, and there were shops, quaint little ones, a row of them on either side of the block—such as it was. The street here was just mud, without even a leavening of gravel, and it ended in a T intersection with an alleyway at the end of the block—if I went straight ahead I'd run smack into a sagging wooden structure that might have been an old garage, or an old barn.

"Here we are!" Mother chirped cheerfully.

I hadn't heard her speak that way in years—decades, really. Startled, I turned to look at her, and she glared back. "Just park the car, Billy boy," she said.

I looked at the street, with its bare mud reaching from doorstep to doorstep across a width of maybe twenty feet, with no sign of sidewalks or curbstones, and decided that one place was as good as another; I stopped the car where it was.It wasn't as if there were any other vehicles in sight. There weren't.

I thought I could feel the car sinking into the mud when I shut off the engine. Certainly, when I got out, I sank into the mud—right to the tops of my shoes.

I'd wondered why Mother was wearing boots when it wasn't raining or snowing; now I knew.I looked around, and I suspect my jaw dropped.

I'm sure you've seen those little mock-colonial neighborhoods, with the mullioned bow windows and the gas streetlights and the brick sidewalks and a bunch of overpriced fake antiques inside, with stick candy in a jar by the cash register. They're big with the tourists; you'll find them all over New England, and scattered through a few other places along the eastern seaboard as well.

I'd thought that was what this place was, when I was driving in, but now that I had a good look—the roof on one shop was thatch. There weren't any streetlights; the lanterns over the doors had candles in them, candles that had actually been lit, going by the smoke-stained glass and the blackened wicks. There weren't any sidewalks, but some shops had planks out to help customers across the gutters. Paint was peeling, bricks were smoked and dirty, glass was cracked—if this was a tourist trap, it was the worst-maintained one I ever saw.

And the signboards, the stuff in the shop windows—it looked real.

"Where are we?" I asked.

"Old Town," Mother said. "Come on." She stomped off at her best pace, which wasn't very good, headed straight toward a shop whose faded signboard read APOTHECARY.

I slogged along behind her; at least I didn't have any trouble keeping up. That would have been embarrassing, given her age.

She scraped her boots on an iron gadget by the shop door, and I tried to do the same, but didn't quite have the hang of it, and damn near pulled one of my loafers off. By the time I had my balance again she was inside and headed straight for the counter, past cabinets full of bottles and displays of weird chemical apparatus.

I hurried after her, across a plank floor that was absolutely black with accumulated grime, and stepped up beside her just as a white-aproned fellow stepped out of the curtained-off back room, took one look at Mother, and said, "'Tis Old Mag, is it? A good day t'ye!"

The phrasing was good old Irish, but the accent wasn't; it sounded almost southern.

"And to you, David Coleman," my mother answered, but she wasn't looking at him, she was rummaging in her purse. "You've more of your remedies, then?" the man asked, leaning forward.

"More of the same, Mr. Coleman." She pulled a little plastic bottle out of her purse, a bottle of big white pills; the label had been peeled off, leaving just a patch of gummy white residue.

"Mother," I whispered, "what is that?"

"It's aspirin, Billy boy—now shut up," she whispered back.

"And is the price the same?" Coleman asked."Unless you'd pay more," Mother snapped back.

"Nay, Old Mag, none of that! I'll pay you a fair price for your witchery, but I'll not be cheated."

"And I won't cheat you. Same price."

Coleman nodded, and reached below the counter. Mother set the bottle on the polished wood, but didn't let go of it.

I didn't know what the hell was going on, so I just watched, and I hoped that stuff really was aspirin. I'd have hated to find out at this late date that my mother was a drug dealer.

Coleman brought up a handful of little round lumps of something and began counting them out onto the counter. At twelve he stopped.

"And there you have it," he said. "A dozen scruples of fine gold."

"Thanks," Mother said, as she carefully scooped up the gold doodads.

"Would you have aught else of me, this fine day?" Coleman asked.

"Don't think so," Mother said. "Been a pleasure doing business with you."

I could just barely keep my mouth shut until we were out the door.

"Mother," I hissed, "why are you selling that man aspirin?"

"They don't have it here," she answered placidly.

"How much is a dozen scruples, anyway?"

"Half an ounce, ninny—didn't anyone ever teach you that in school?"

"No, they..."I stopped in my tracks. "Mother," I said.

"What is it, Billy?"

"Half an ounce of gold is about a hundred and fifty dollars, isn't it?"

"About that," she agreed. "Except this is avoirdupois, and they figure gold in troy. Figure a hundred and twenty."

"For a bottle of aspirin?"

"They don't have it here, Billy. Now, come on."

Utterly confused, halfway certain I'd just seen my mother sell a hundred tablets of cocaine or something equally illegal, I followed her across the street to the car. I opened the door for her, but then asked, "Where are we, that they don't have aspirin?"

She shrugged. "I told you, Billy," she said. "Old Town."

Before I could say anything else, a voice cried, "Old Mag!"

Mother turned, and so did I.

There was a woman standing in the street, hands on her hips, glaring at us. She was a handsome creature, rather gypsyish—dark-haired, medium height, medium build, hair pulled back in a long, thick braid, wearing a white blouse and a brown ankle-length skirt. She could have been anywhere from twenty-five to fifty.

I stared, I admit it. She was worth staring at."Jenny McGill," Mother said. "What do you want?"

"You know what I want, Old Mag," the woman answered. "I'd have seen the last of you, that's what I want!"

"Oh, come on," Mother said. "I'm eighty-three years old next month, I'll be dead soon, you can't let me do a little business here while I last?"

"Ha!" The McGill woman tossed her head theatrically. "Your kind can't be trusted to die a decent death, and I've had enough of waiting!"

"So don't wait. I come here what, once a week, and sell Davey Coleman a few things?"

"Mother..." I began.

"Shut up, Billy," Mother muttered.

"Old Mag, I told you when last you came, there's no room for two witches in Old Town, and 'tis my place, not yours! We need no outsiders here."

"I've been coming here sixty years, since before your mother was born, you call me an outsider?" Mother called back. "Jenny McGill, you mind your manners! Your mother never spoke to me like that, rest her dear soul." She climbed into the car.

I hesitated, looking at Mother, then at Jenny McGill.

"Close the door, Billy, let's get going," Mother said.

I shut the door, and started around to the driver's side, but before I got there Jenny McGill came striding up.

I started to say something, to apologize for my mother, but before I got a word out she put a hand on either side of my head and pulled me down and kissed me.

Wow.

I've been married twice, and had a few flings, and I figured I knew the basics, but I had never been kissed like that. I mean, I popped right to attention, so to speak, thought I might tear my pants, I was sweating and trembling and half-blind, couldn't see anything but those dark eyes...

"Take your hands off him, Jenny," my mother called, leaning out the car window.

Jenny stopped kissing me, but she kept her hands right where they were. "Never before were you so foolish as to bring a man," she called back. "You know where my powers lie, yet your chosen companion this time's a man in his prime—you've grown old and foolish, Old Mag, and I've got you this time."

"Jenny McGill, you take your hands off my son," Mother called.

She had been bringing her lips up for another kiss, but at the word "son" she froze, and stared up into my eyes.

I wasn't thinking any too clearly, but I had an armful of woman, and I did the natural thing—I started to lean down to meet her halfway with that kiss.

She screamed, and tried to pull free, and my hands slipped, and she plopped backward into the mud.

"Your son!" she shrieked. "You...I...Old Mag, forgive me, I didn't..."

"Get in the car," Mother snapped.

I got in the car."Drive," she said.

"But she's still in front of us."

"Drive," Mother said, in a tone of voice I remembered from childhood—remembered with considerable dread.

I drove.

Jenny McGill rolled out of the way, and by the time I realized I was heading toward that T intersection at the end of the block she was on her feet again, dripping mud, shouting after us and waving her fist.

"It's going to be tough turning around here," I said. "The street's pretty narrow..."

"Are you crazy?" Mother said. "We're not turning around; she's still back there, and any minute now she's going to realize that even if you are my son, you don't have any more of the Talent than a cabbage. If you did, she'd have felt it when she kissed you."

"But then where..."

"Through there," Mother said, pointing.

The door of that garage, or barn, or whatever it was, was opening.

I didn't know what else to do; I drove through.

The interior was dark; I could just barely make out a dusty interior, strange machinery like antique farm equipment along either side, and a ramp straight ahead that ran down out of sight, down into more complete darkness.

I headed down the ramp. I turned on the headlights, and saw nothing but hard-packed brown earth, underneath us and to either side. Whatever was above us was invisible in the gloom.

"Where are we going?" I asked.

"Down," Mother said.

That wasn't much help, but I drove on in silence for a moment. The ramp kept on going down, between those two walls, deeper into the darkness.

After awhile I'd had enough, though. "Mother," I said, slowing the car a little, "What the hell is going on?"

"I'm trying to get a little shopping done, that's all," Mother said defensively. "It's not my fault Jenny McGill's got too big for her britches, wanting to keep Old Town all for herself."

"She said you're a witch."

Mother shrugged.

"Mother," I said, "what is this Old Town place? I never heard of it, never saw it before. How can they have witches there? Nobody believes in witches any more. Why don't they have aspirin?"

"Never invented it, I guess," she said.

"And witches?"

She shrugged again. "I know a few things," she said. "They want to call it witchcraft, what do I care?"

"But what is Old Town?"

"It's a place, all right? You think every place there is gets on the maps, every place has TV and telephones?"

Well, in fact I thought exactly that, but I decided not to say so. "It seems kind of backward," I said.

"It's different, all right," she agreed—if it was agreement. "Good place for leather goods and ironmongery, and I can usually do someone a favor there for a little spending money."

It was getting stuffy in the car; I flicked on the air conditioning. I thought I saw a faint orange glow ahead, though it was hard to be sure with the headlights on.

"Listen," Mother said, "we're going to come out in a big cave in a few minutes, and when we do you want to take the second tunnel on the right—got that? Second on the right."

"Yes, Mother," I said.

She hadn't mentioned that the cave would be so sweltering hot that the air shimmered and the windows were hot to the touch; the car's air conditioner was struggling along as best it could, but I was sweating and the steering wheel was sticky.

She also didn't mention the bright orange glare that came from somewhere off to the left, down below the road, where I couldn't see whatever produced it. She didn't mention that we'd be on a narrow road along the top of a cliff, with no railing, just a sheer drop. And she didn't mention the things that were watching us from niches in the far wall, on the other side of the chasm.

If Mother hadn't said anything I'd have taken that first right, to get the hell out of that place, but I held on another hundred feet and took the second right, into the welcome darkness of another tunnel; this one, thank heavens, was heading upward, rather than further down.

Unfortunately, it wasn't as nice and straight as the one that led down from Old Town. It wiggled and wound its way upward, and twice I heard metal scraping on rock as I squeezed the car around those narrow turns.

"I don't usually come this way," Mother remarked."I can see why not," I said, as I negotiated another curve.

"Mary's Cadillac won't fit through here at all; I'm glad you've got a sensible car."

Mother's friend Mary has a '73 Eldorado. "I like to be able to park," I said.

Then the tunnel ended—the headlights illuminated a pair of heavy wooden doors, instead of more rock. I barely stopped in time.

"The bar's on this side," Mother said. "You'll have to open them."

I squeezed out of the car, lifted the bar, and pushed the doors open; sunlight poured in. I blinked and looked around, and saw forest. "Where are we?" I asked.

"Come on, get in the car," Mother called.

We got rolling again, down a dirt road that wound through woods, past some of the biggest trees I've ever seen in my life—not giant redwoods or anything, but oaks and chestnuts that would've considered a sixty-footer a hopeless runt.

"I wasn't planning to come this way," Mother said, "but as long as we're here, take a left at the fork."

I took a left, and then... Then I don't remember what happened next, but I was driving through the woods again, the sun was lower in the sky by at least an hour, and there was a bolt of fabric on the back seat.

I looked at Mother, at the fabric—lovely stuff, patterned silk— and then at the road, and decided not to ask about it.

"Where now?" I asked.

"Right," she said, pointing, and a few minutes later we came out of the woods onto the shoulder of the interstate a mile outside town. I got on the highway.

"D'you know where Stilson Jewelers is?"

"I think so," I said.

"Well, go there—I'm going to sell Mr. Coleman's gold, and then you can take me to Aubrey's Foodliner and we'll get the groceries."

I waited in the car while she sold the gold, and while I waited I thought about it all. This had been, without a doubt, the weirdest day of my life—but it was fascinating, too. That forest was beautiful, and I had a feeling that whatever I didn't remember there had been pleasant, and driving the tunnels was exciting, and Old Town had a certain charm to it.

A large part of that charm was Jenny McGill, I had to admit—she was a fine-looking woman, no question about it.

Of course, she was apparently ready to kill my mother and me on sight, but still, remembering her had a certain thrill. Maybe it was witchcraft, or maybe I just hadn't been kissed by enough pretty women lately.

And of course, there was the mystery of where those places were. They didn't seem to connect. There weren't any woods like that along the interstate, I'd have sworn to it, and I never saw anything like Old Town before—remembering the route, I thought we should have come out behind the old railroad station, not on a block of shops left from some other century.

But did I think every place there is gets on the maps, that every place has TV and telephones? I'd always loved stories of secret rooms and hidden passages when I was a kid—maybe I'd just found the grown-up equivalent.

"Mother," I asked, when she was back in the car, "how'd you find these places?"

She didn't pretend to misunderstand. "You've just gotta know how to look, Billy boy," she said. "And I've been at it a long, long time. Since before you were born."

"Why'd you never take me along?"

She sighed. "Two reasons—maybe more. First, a boy child's a little too valuable in some of them, a little too tempting. You wouldn't leave one of those boomboxes on the car seat down on East Main Street while you were shopping, would you?"

I had to admit that I wouldn't.

"Second, I didn't suppose you'd appreciate it. You were always such a sober little kid, no sign of the Talent at all—why confuse you with a bunch of places you'd probably never see again?"

I could see that. I didn't think it was right, not really—but I was never the life of any party, never had much of a creative flair for anything. Whatever fantasy life I might have never showed much— I never let it. Hell, my first wife left me because I was boring. I've known for a long time that people didn't find me fascinating.

Even my own mother.

I thought about that while I pushed the cart through the supermarket for her.

I wasn't as boring as all that. I had an imagination. It just didn't show.

And this Talent that Mother talked about—what was it?

Did I have it after all, maybe? That kiss might have told more than Mother knew.

"That Jenny McGill..." I began.

"That bitch," Mother snapped. "See if I go back there again! Someone else can bring them their aspirin and penicillin from now on!"

I thought about that on the way back to Mother's house.

By the next week, I was back home and Mother's friends were driving her again.

But a month later I wangled a transfer to Boston. I said I wanted to be nearer Mother, in case her health went, and the home office didn't mind. I bought a condo a mile from Mother's house and commuted into the city five days a week.

On weekends I just drove around town. Alone, not with Mother.

It took me six weeks and a dozen tries before I found Old Town again. It took me an hour of fast talk and dodging before Jenny McGill would listen to what I had to say.

Finding the place got easier every time, though, and really, Jenny can be perfectly reasonable when she wants to.

She doesn't think I'm boring. I courted her for six months, and at last she gave in. We've posted the banns, and she and Mother have declared an armed truce. Mother still won't go back to Old Town, but I've brought Jenny to dinner a few times. Maybe I'm under a spell; if so, I don't care. Witch or not, she's a fine woman.

And I've found a few shortcuts. There are a lot of places that aren't on the maps. Whatever happens now, it won't be boring.

Mother always did know the best places to shop.

Jim Tuckerman's Angel

Jim Tuckerman wanted to see angels more than he wanted anything else on God's green earth.

He couldn't easily explain why. When his friends or family would ask him what was so goddamned special about angels, he got tongue-tied and awkward, but would eventually, with the proper coaxing, manage a few fragmentary sentences about how glorious God's own messengers must be, and how wonderful it was that God sent them among ordinary folks.

Whereupon Jim's mother would either sniff disdainfully or growl angrily, depending on her mood, and point out that the Good Book said that God had created *Man* in His own image, and while Man had fallen from his high estate back when Eve pussywhipped Adam into eating the wrong thing, it still seemed to her that angels that were created just as God's errand boys wouldn't be half so magnificent as a good-looking young man in tight jeans.

"Bunch of half-assed things, neither man nor woman," she said. "You want to see folks can't make up their mind whether they're pitching or catching, you just go on out to San Francisco and cruise the streets a bit, you'll see plenty. And I figure angels probably aren't much better. You'll notice God never wastes much time talking to *them* in the Bible; no, He knows that men are a hell of a lot more interesting, got more *to* 'em, than the bunch of dickless choirboys He's got fetchin' and carryin' for Him!"

"The Bible's for men and women, Ma," Jim said. "That's why it's about us and not the angels. They don't *need* an instruction book to know what God wants of them; they're God's will made manifest. That's why I want to see 'em, meet them and talk with them; they know God better than we do."

"Hmph."

Jim didn't try to convince his mother of anything; he knew her better than that. She'd settled her mind on its path a long time ago, probably when he was still in diapers, and he couldn't see her turning aside from it for anything short of the Second Coming— and at least she wasn't expecting that to happen next Tuesday, the way Aunt Aimee was.

But he wasn't letting her turn *him* aside, either. He looked around at the world God had created, the cast-aside world that God had left to Adam and Eve after they disappointed Him so much, and he saw the glory and wonder of it all, the magnificence of the vast blue sky and the bright green leaves, the smell of woodsmoke or wisteria or a pretty woman, the sound of the birds in the trees and the water in the creek, and it was all so beautiful he could scarcely stand it—and this was the *fallen* world, while the Lord's angels never fell. How much more beautiful would they be, then?

Jim knew that for a lot of folks, God and His angels were something you talked about on Sunday mornings that didn't have a thing to do with the everyday world. But Jim didn't see it that way. He knew other people didn't see any angels, but he didn't let that stop him. He was pretty sure, from what the other fellows said, that he saw things not everyone saw—that he saw *more* than most people. He hoped that meant that he might be able to see an angel where other men wouldn't, because he *needed* to see one.

Angels were the only glimpse of Heaven a man could hope for while he lived, and Jim wasn't anywhere near sure enough of himself to think he'd be seeing anything but flames once he died. He knew he was a shiftless fool, since everyone had told him as much every day of his life, and he didn't see as how there'd be room for such a one in God's Heaven. Oh, Jesus loved him, he knew that, had been told it since before he could talk, but Jim didn't figure that meant he wouldn't catch Hell for his sins when he died, any more than old Ticker hadn't caught Hell from Jim when he'd dig out under the fence to chase rabbits. Despite that Jim loved the old dog, he'd whacked Ticker across the nose and tied him up when he misbehaved and left him to whimper, and Jim wasn't expecting anything kinder from God when his time came. A man should know better than a dog how to behave.

With that in mind, Jim didn't think he'd be singing hymns in Heaven for eternity. He was pretty sure he was bound the other way. He accepted that, but before he went he wanted to get a look at what he'd be missing, and here on Earth that could only mean an angel.

He didn't explain this all to his friends, for fear they'd tell him what a fool he was. He'd been talked out of a good many things in his life, and usually he wished later that he hadn't been, and he wasn't going to let that happen with this. It was too important. It was so important, in fact, that he didn't intend to just quietly wait around home in hopes an angel would stop by Ballard, Kentucky on business. He intended to go out looking for one.

He didn't tell his friends *that*, either.

Angels went everywhere, of course, going about the Lord's business; everyone had a guardian angel watching over him. That was what Preacher Bill said, and Jim had never heard anyone question it. God's messengers had errands to attend to in every corner of the world.

Jim hadn't seen any of them, though, and he'd been looking. He wasn't sure whether they were invisible even to him, or moved so quick he never caught a glimpse of them, or watched from afar with telescopic vision like Superman in the comics, but he never saw them.

He wanted to see one. It wasn't enough to know they were there; he wanted to *see* one.

He'd tried praying for a glimpse, but as yet he hadn't got an answer, unless the answer was "no." God helps those who help themselves, though, so he wasn't going to just wait. He was going looking.

He'd thought it out. Angels were God's messengers, watching over people. Didn't it follow, then, that there'd be more angels, and more of a chance of seeing one, if he was somewhere with more *people* in it? Ballard, population 115, was not exactly bustling.

So one day in August he drove the old Dodge 150 out of the barn, called to his mother, "Goin' into town, Ma. Not sure when I'll be back," and headed up the highway past Winchester to the interstate. He had a few hundred dollars he'd saved up stuffed in his pants, and a bag of clothes and the like tossed in the back of the pick-up, and when he got to I-64 he headed east, because everyone knew it was more crowded back east on the coast than it was anywhere else.

It didn't *look* more crowded at first, there where I-64 headed up into the mountains and through the Daniel Boone National Forest, but he knew he'd get to the real east eventually, and come out in Washington or New York or someplace like that.

He drove up past Ashland and Huntington and on to the east, staying on I-64 clear across West Virginia and into Virginia, where I-81 came in from the south. He drove past mile upon mile of rich green country, tall straight trees and fine green fields, all washed in God's golden sunlight, and he marveled at the beauty of it all. The world was lush and lovely, and he gloried in it as he drove.

When I-64 split off from I-81 again and turned toward Richmond he stayed on I-81, because the signs said that could get him to Washington DC, and he thought that if ever there was a place on God's Earth that needed angels, it must be Washington.

Those senators and presidential staffers and all surely needed the Lord's guidance to keep God's country in its proper order, and wouldn't there be angels to bring that guidance to hand?

By then he'd driven the day through. The sky was dark now, and he was tired, and the right headlight on the Dodge didn't work the way it ought, so he followed the signs to a motel in New Market and got himself a room, and bought himself supper at the family diner across the road.

After he'd eaten he went back to the motel and sat in his room reading the Bible—the story of Lot, mostly. When he finished the chapter he said his prayers and went to bed.

In the morning he got up and got himself showered and dressed, and went out to the Dodge with his bag in one hand, but he didn't get behind the wheel right at the first, because there was a man on the ground between Jim's pick-up and the next car over, which was an old blue Chevy with taped-on plastic where the passenger side window should have been. The man had one hand under the Chevy, and his head pushed up to the underside of the Chevy.

He looked up at the sound of Jim's footsteps, and Jim recognized his face as one he'd seen at supper the night before. It was a handsome face, with a narrow jaw and deep-set eyes.

"Got some trouble there?" Jim asked.

"'Fraid I do," the man said. "The engine turns over fine, but there's no power to the wheels. I was thinkin' it might be a busted driveshaft."

"More like to be the transmission gone bad," Jim said. "Not that that's so very much better."

"You're probably right about that," the man said. He glanced at the Dodge. "That your truck?"

"Yessir."

"And I'm blockin' you, aren't I? Sorry 'bout that." He rolled over and sat up. Then he looked up at Jim again from where he sat. "You wouldn't happen to be on your way to DC, would you?"

"I might be," Jim admitted. "Why?"

"I got no right to ask you this, and if it's any bother you just tell me no, but I sure could use a lift. I've got a job interview in Washington this afternoon, and there's no way *this* heap is gonna get me there." He slapped the Chevy. "Probably be a week's work to get her runnin' again, and that's assuming they can get the parts and they'll trust me to pay 'em, which frankly, *I* wouldn't. Hell, the repairs are probably gonna cost more than the damn thing's worth." He got to his feet, and said, "What do you say?"

Jim had to think about this a little. Ma had always told him he was too trusting of strangers, but giving a man a helping hand was the Christian thing to do, and it wasn't as if Jim had anything much this fellow was likely to be after stealing. The Dodge was in better shape than the Chevy, but not by much, and the stranger couldn't know about the cash in Jim's pants; if he was looking to rob someone, he wouldn't have picked Jim.

He wasn't any sort of pervert or anything, either, Jim was pretty sure. He didn't look a bit like Ma's descriptions; wasn't a touch of make-up on him, and his clothes were just good decent clothes, no leather or silk.

And it could be that the Lord had put this man in his path for a reason. After all, God knew what Jim was up to, and why wouldn't He want to give Jim a hand? Sure, Jim was hellbound, but that didn't mean God wouldn't cut him a break while Jim was still drawing breath. Jesus loved him, after all.

"I could do that," Jim said.

"Awright! *Thank* you, friend! I'll pay my share of the gas. Let me get my gear and turn in my key, and we can go soon as you're ready."

"All right. I'll be turning in my key, too." Jim had been thinking about maybe getting himself some breakfast, but now he thought he'd put that off a bit.

Jim tossed his bag in the back of the Dodge, then went back to check on his room and make sure he hadn't left anything; then he went to the office to drop off the key, and got there just as the other man stepped up to the counter.

A moment later the two of them walked out to the truck together. The rider tossed his big old backpack in the back, next to Jim's bag, then held out a hand and said, "My name's Nick Lichtman."

"Jim," Jim said, shaking the offered hand quick and firm.

Then the two headed for the two doors. Jim climbed behind the wheel, while Nick slid into the passenger seat. "It's real generous of you to give me a lift," Nick said. "I could really use this job."

"It's not so much," Jim said. "What line of work are you in?"

"Reclamation," Nick said. "Been working freelance these last few years, but I'm hoping to get a government job—I wouldn't mind having a pension and a health plan. What about you?"

"My folks have been farming for nigh onto a hundred years, out in Ballard, Kentucky," Jim said. "Corn and tobacco, mostly." He started the engine.

"A son of the soil, huh? Lot of hard work, farming."

"Can be," Jim acknowledged, as he shifted into reverse.

"So what takes you to the nation's capital?"

Jim concentrated on getting out of the parking space and didn't answer.

Nick seemed to take the hint, and shut up, at least for the moment. He let Jim get out of the parking lot and up the state road and onto the interstate in peace.

That seemed to be all the quiet he could stand, though. "Where you bound in DC?" he asked. "My interview's on 14th Street, right downtown."

"Don't rightly know," Jim said, concentrating on the traffic. He wasn't used to driving as fast as folks did on this side of the mountains.

"You're not after work, then? Nor visiting family?"

"Nope."

"Not much of a talker, are you?" he said.

Jim glanced at him. "Don't suppose I've much to say just now," he said. "I'm keeping my mind on the driving."

"In my experience, a man who don't talk's got something he wants to keep to himself, and he's afraid it'll slip out if he opens his mouth."

"Can't say as that's been *my* experience. Might be any number of reasons to keep a mouth shut." He glanced at the eighteen-wheeler in the rear view mirror; it was coming up fast behind them, and he wasn't sure whether he'd best get out of its way, or just let it pass.

"But when a man answers a civil question with a bunch of dodges, I think there's something he doesn't want to say. Why *are* you going to Washington?"

"Don't see as it's any of your business," Jim said.

"It's not, but you're doin' me a favor as it is, I know that, so I was thinkin' I might do you one in return. You said you didn't know just where you were going in Washington; if you tell me what you're after, I might be able to help you out with that. I've been there before, know the city pretty well. I can tell you the best route to the White House, if that's what you want to see."

"It's not."

"But you're lookin' for *something*, aren't you?"

Jim sighed. "I am," he admitted.

"What is it?"

Jim remembered his earlier thought, that the Lord might have put this fellow Nick in his path for a reason. Besides, what was he going to do if he thought Jim was crazy? He was in Jim's truck, after all, and the .38 under the seat was on Jim's side.

"I'm looking for an angel," he said.

Nick considered that carefully for a moment before replying. He looked Jim over, then looked out the windshield at the highway for a bit, then looked at Jim again.

"There's them that if they said that, I'd think they meant someone with money to invest, but you don't strike me as that kind," Nick said. "There's them I'd think meant they were lookin' to get laid, but you don't seem one of those, either. I'm thinkin' you mean it just the way you said it—you want to see one of God's own angels, and not any sort of human being at all."

"That's right," Jim said, a trifle uneasy at how Nick was taking this.

"Not a dead friend or relative?"

Jim snorted. "Dead souls ain't angels," he said. "Anyone who thinks that ain't read the Good Book or paid attention in Bible school. The dead in Heaven are saints, not angels. Angels are God's messengers, made before Man."

Nick nodded and looked out at the road again. "I know that. Just makin' sure you did."

"'Course I do."

The eighteen-wheeler roared past them in the left lane, and Jim gripped the wheel to keep the Dodge straight on the highway.

A moment later Nick said, "How do you know *haven't* seen an angel?"

"What?"

"Well, they can look human if they want to, can't they? That's in the Bible, that some have entertained angels unawares. And the ones who visited Lot in Sodom, they were beautiful, but the Sodomites thought they were human."

Jim frowned, remembering what he'd read the night before. Nick was right, but still...

"Then I haven't seen an angel, have I? Just an angel's disguise."

"It's still an angel."

"It's not what I'm looking for."

"So you want to look on beauty bare, is that it?"

Jim glanced at him. "You could say that," he said.

"Are you sure? Remember that a lot of the angels in the Bible were terrible to look upon—half the time the first thing they say is 'Fear not.' You really want a look at something like that?"

"Yes, I truly do," Jim said, letting up on the gas so as not to gain on the eighteen-wheeler on the upgrade they'd just hit.

"Why?"

"Because I reckon it's the closest I'll ever get to looking on the face of God."

Nick didn't answer that right away, but just looked at Jim, his expression growing thoughtful.

"Not optimistic about your post-mortem prospects, I take it?"

Jim glanced at him. "What?"

"Not expecting anything good when you die?"

Jim looked back at the road before answering. This fellow was smart, maybe smarter than Jim entirely liked.

"No reason I should," he said.

Nick nodded. "Well, you'd know that better than I."

For a moment neither man spoke; then Nick asked, "Why Washington?"

"It's a big city. Lots for angels to do."

"You think more people means a better chance of findin' an angel? Seems to me that's huntin' a needle in a haystack."

"God's got a plan for us all," Jim said. "Seems to me He'd send His angels to keep an eye on that plan."

"God sees every sparrow's fall, though. He and His angels would be everywhere."

"Not that I've seen. People have guardian angels, though. I reckon if I get around enough people, I've got a better chance of spotting me an angel."

Nick considered that for a moment, then shook his head. "I don't think it works like that. I never heard of anyone seein' guardian angels in New York, 'less you mean those punks with the berets."

"I wouldn't know about that," Jim said. "But if I don't look in the cities, where *do* I look?"

"I don't know," Nick admitted. "I never heard of anyone went lookin' for angels and found 'em. I'm not sure you *can* see 'em." He grimaced. "Not what you wanted to hear, I suppose."

"Can't say that it is. But I see things other folks don't, sometimes, so I'm thinking I might see an angel if there's one to be seen."

"But you haven't seen one yet."

"Nope."

"So you don't know if you can?"

"Not for certain, but my heart says I can."

They drove on in silence for some time then, making the turn to the east onto I-66 through Front Royal. They'd gone another ten miles when Nick spoke.

"Seems to me," he said suddenly, "that you gotta look at this logically. You been thinkin' about guardian angels, but hardly anyone ever seen one of those, at least not and known it. But there's other angels."

"Don't know how to find them either, though," Jim said gloomily.

"But there's one angel that you know where he's gonna be, sooner or later. And it's one that doesn't bother with disguises."

Jim glanced at him. "There is?"

"The angel of death."

Jim didn't answer right away; he took his time to think about that.

Finally, though, he said, "No man knows the hour of his passing, so where do you reckon I'd find the Angel of Death?"

"A hospital," Nick said. "The terminal ward. Maybe the emergency room."

Jim considered that long and hard, and had to admit there was some promise to the idea.

"You don't hear much about people seein' the angel of death in the E.R.," Nick mused, "but then, they aren't lookin'."

"Might be there's a good reason for that."

"People don't much like to think about death, that's for sure."

That wasn't what Jim had meant, but he didn't say so.

They drove on in silence again for some time after that.

Finally, though, as they were cutting through Arlington and the Washington Monument was just visible ahead on the left, gleaming white in the sun, Jim said, "I don't suppose you'd know much about hospitals in Washington?"

"Not a lot," Nick admitted. "There's one at Georgetown University." He pointed past the monument.

Jim nodded. "Where'd you say your appointment is at?"

"Fourteenth Street, just across the bridge. Stay straight on this highway across the river—it changes number, but don't let that throw you, and as soon as you're across the river the highway curves to the right, but you bear left onto Independence Avenue and then turn left again onto 14th, and it's just a few blocks up."

A few minutes later they were indeed on Independence Avenue, and Jim saw a sign for 14th Street. They were driving through the largest city Jim had ever seen. "It looks like something off the television," he said.

"Well, yeah," Nick said. "Can you pull over up ahead there? I think that's the building." He pointed.

Jim managed to maneuver the Dodge over to the curb without causing a collision or encouraging much honking, and let Nick out. He fetched his pack from the back, then leaned back in and said, "Thanks for the ride. You serious about findin' a hospital?"

"Reckon I am."

"Well, if you go on up 14th across the Mall, then turn left on Pennsylvania Avenue up ahead, that'll take you into Georgetown, and maybe there'll be signs."

"I'll give it a try, then. Good luck." He waved, and pulled back into traffic.

When he looked back on it later, Jim was amazed he managed to get anywhere in that city without getting the pick-up's fenders more banged up than they already were. There were more cars in every block than in all of Ballard, more on every street than he'd seen in all his life, and about half of them were apparently being driven by crazies. Somehow, though, he got through it without hitting a thing.

He thought maybe his own personal guardian angel might have a thing or two to do with it, but he never did see any such being. If there was an angel at work, it was doing its best to stay out of sight. God's handiwork wasn't so obvious as that here. Man's creations were everywhere, but except for a few trees and the sky above, the hand of the Lord was less evident.

But God had created Man in His image, and that image was everywhere. The streets were crowded with more people than Jim had ever seen. It was greatly distracting, and it took him more than an hour to find his way from one blue H sign to the next and finally to a hospital.

He wasn't entirely sure whether this was the Georgetown University one that Nick had mentioned, or another, but it didn't much matter—it was a hospital. He found a place to park the Dodge and walked into the hospital lobby.

There he stopped to look around, wondering where he might best go to have a chance of seeing the Angel of Death. No man knows the hour of his passing, as he'd told Nick, but Jim was sure that in a big place like this, full of the sick and injured, someone must die pretty much every day, and it was just a matter of finding the right person and staying by him until the Angel came for him.

There was a directory on the wall near the elevators; Jim went to take a look. He thought the cancer ward might be a good place to start, but when he read the list he didn't see cancer; he saw any number of long names he didn't know, like endocrinology and oncology, and he guessed one of those must be a doctor's word for cancer, but he didn't know which.

But there was an emergency room, and that was probably as good a place as any to look.

He almost expected someone to stop him and ask what he was doing there, or demand to see a visitor's badge, or some such a thing, but no one did; he walked down the corridor and through the sliding glass door into the emergency room and looked around.

There were empty beds in darkened alcoves, and people in beds behind screens or curtains, and doctors and nurses dressed in white. It was quiet—not at all like the emergency rooms he had seen on TV, but of course those had been made-up stories about exciting times, not about ordinary days.

He stood for awhile, trying to decide what he should do. He felt a bit like a vulture, standing there hoping someone would die; it didn't seem right.

But then, maybe he might see another sort of angel here. Guardian angels must be busy in a place like this. He found a chair in an open area and sat for a time, taking it in, listening to the murmur of the nurses' voices, and the louder words of the doctors, and the tapping of fingers on keyboards, and looking around, trying to understand what he was seeing.

No one troubled him; they were all busy with their own concerns and none of his.

After a time—he wasn't sure how long, but it might've been an hour—he grew restless. He had been sitting there waiting for something to happen, and it wasn't any better than waiting back home in Ballard. He got back on his feet and began walking along, looking at each occupied bed, or at the screens and curtains, hoping for some sign of God's messengers.

As he did, a doctor hurried past, and then another, and he turned to see that they were gathering at the big glass door where a sign read AMBULANCE ENTRANCE—STAND CLEAR.

Then he heard a siren, and the roar of an engine, and the squeal of tires, as the door slid open, and a big boxy red ambulance was pulling up, the doctors hurrying out to meet it. Men in heavy coats swung open the rear doors and began hauling out stretchers. Jim stared, his heart in his throat, as three stretchers were unloaded, their wheels unfolded, and then they were rolling into the emergency room, and a nurse was suddenly at his elbow asking, "Can I help you find someone, sir?"

"No," Jim said, keeping his gaze fixed on the stretchers. "I was... I was on my way out and I saw..."

"Don't get in anyone's way," the nurse said. Then she was hurrying toward the stretchers herself.

Two of the stretchers had been rolled away already, but the third was still by the door, with people clustered around it and doctors bent over, and then it was there, above the stretcher. Jim saw it, and he knew instantly what he was seeing.

The Angel of Death.

It was a darkness and emptiness that filled the room without being in it at all. It had no shape but it had great black colorless wings and blind, all-seeing eyes. For an instant Jim saw it, saw the utter all-consuming nothingness of it, like an endless hole in the universe, there above the body.

And beyond it, *through* it, so briefly that Jim could not be sure he really saw anything at all, was something that might have been a light, or might have been nothing at all.

Then it was gone, and the doctors were stepping away from the body, and someone was swearing repetitiously, saying the same two words over and over, and Jim felt tears on his cheeks.

He stared at the place where the angel had been.

It had been so *quick*. He hadn't had anything like a good look at it.

He had seen an angel, right enough, but he hadn't seen *enough* of it. He wanted a good hard look at it.

The stretcher with the corpse on it was rolled away, out of his sight somewhere, and the doctors were gone with it, and Jim stood staring at the big glass door. It had closed again, and the big red ambulance had driven away, without sirens or lights.

He reached up and dabbed at his eyes, blinking away the tears.

"Did you see what you came for?" a voice asked, a familiar voice, and Jim turned to see Nick Lichtman standing there behind him.

"Reckon I did," Jim said. "What brings *you* here? Wa'n't you getting interviewed?"

"I got interviewed," Nick said. "They said to come back tomorrow, ten a.m., for a follow-up, which is promisin', but it left me a bit at loose ends for the rest of today, y'know? So I thought I'd come see if you found the place and got what you were after."

"I found it," Jim said.

"Did you see your angel?"

"I saw it."

Nick blinked. "Did you really?"

"I saw it," Jim repeated, remembering that vast dark emptiness, and the tantalizing hint of something more, something *beyond*.

Nick stared at him. "I will be damned," he said. "What did it look like?"

"Can't rightly say. Big. Dark. Empty."

"That doesn't sound real attractive."

Jim looked at Nick the way he'd look at a hound that wouldn't back down when called off. "I wouldn't think the Angel of *Death* ought to be real pretty," he said.

But even as he said it, he knew he was wrong. The angel had been beautiful in its utter desolation, in its purity and simplicity. There were no complications to it, no uncertainties—it was exactly and entirely what it was, no more and no less, without doubts or reservations. Jim remembered his mother talking about the glories of a man's body, and he supposed she had a point; certainly a *woman's* body was beautiful in its complexity and contradictions, the combinations of softness and strength, the smooth surfaces that were actually an intricate mass of fluids and follicles and a hundred other things.

The angel had had none of that, no flesh, no real shape, nothing but a single iteration of divine will, absolute and infinite, and it had been terrible and beautiful.

Jim ached to look on it again, to drink in the sight of that essence.

"I suppose not," Nick said. "Nothin' pretty about death. So you're satisfied? Ready to go back home to Kentucky?"

"No," Jim said slowly. "Can't say I am." He wanted to see it again. He wanted to see what lay beyond it, whether there was really anything there at all, or whether he had imagined that because his mind could not comprehend so total an emptiness.

"No?" Nick looked around the emergency room. "What are you thinkin'?"

"It was too quick," Jim said. "I didn't get a good look at it. And it was almost like I could see something *through* it." The words didn't convey his meaning well, but human speech couldn't.

Nick's expression turned suddenly solemn. "Through it?"

"Yup."

"You don't just mean the wall, do you?"

"No." Whatever he had or hadn't seen within and beyond the angel, it was nothing there in the emergency room.

"Was it... you know, the light? *The* light?"

"Might've been. Couldn't say for sure." Jim hadn't really thought about it in those terms. To reduce whatever he had glimpsed to human words like light, or Heaven, or Hell, or even the Face of God, seemed to diminish it somehow.

"You *saw* it?"

"Can't say for sure. Thought I might've."

"You mean it? You aren't pullin' my leg?"

"I'm not joking." Jim's expression left no room for doubt.

For a moment the two men stood silently thinking. Then Nick said, "There's some would say you must be nuts."

Jim smiled crookedly. "It's a sad world, my Ma says, where people don't know what they're seeing, and if seeing angels means I'm crazy, I'd say she was right—that's pretty sad. The Bible talks about people seeing angels, and people have seen 'em all along, now and again. I don't reckon one's got to be crazy."

"Most people don't see angels."

"Most people aren't looking."

"So you saw the Angel of Death, and you want another look at it?"

"That's about the way of it."

"What're you goin' to do about it?"

"Hadn't made up my mind as yet."

"Gonna wait around here until someone else dies?" Nick glanced around at the quiet room—there were voices from somewhere off to the left, where the doctors were working on the others who'd been brought in by that ambulance, but this area was deserted for the moment. "Could take awhile."

"It could," Jim agreed.

Nick looked around again, then leaned close and whispered, "O'course, you could hurry things up a little."

Jim blinked. "What?" Astonished, he looked at Nick's face.

"You could find some poor bastard who hasn't got very long and help him along," Nick said quietly. "Maybe a pillow over the face. So you won't blink at the wrong time, or be in the john when it happens. Be a shame to sit with someone for days waiting for him to die, and then miss the show."

"You...you're saying I might kill someone?" The idea was horrible—but at the same time, the idea of seeing the Angel of Death again was horribly alluring.

It was a temptation, truly it was. Jim look at Nick.

"Someone who's dying anyway," Nick said. "You'd be putting him out of his misery, y'know? It'd be a kindness, really."

Jim looked into Nick's eyes—brown eyes, dark and deep-set. Jim looked into those eyes long and hard, and he saw what there was to see there, and he shivered.

He saw emptiness there, and darkness, and a deliberate hiding of any light that might lie beyond. There was a purity and simplicity to that darkness that was not quite like anything Jim had ever seen in a man's eyes before.

He remembered his mother saying that men were more interesting than angels, that there was more *to* them, and he knew she'd been right.

"It's not for us to play God," Jim said.

"What?" Nick said, backing off a little from Jim's gaze. "Okay, maybe that's not such a great idea, killing someone, but just waiting..."

"You can stop now," Jim said, interrupting him and looking away.

"What?"

"I know you. I've seen enough." Jim looked up at the ceiling, at the off-white acoustic tile.

"Jim, I'm just tryin' to be helpful..."

"You're tempting me, Nick, and I don't want that. I've seen enough. I'll be going home now." He started to turn away.

Nick caught his arm. "Home? But you wanted another look at the Angel of Death!"

"Reckon I've seen enough angels for now," Jim said. "More than my share, I'm thinking."

"One quick look at the Angel of Death?" Nick sounded almost angry. "That's enough for you? I thought you'd said you'd been waitin' all your life to see and angel, and you get half a glimpse, and you're ready to pack it up and go home?"

"I've had more than a glimpse," Jim said. "Seems to me I drove halfway across Virginia with an angel beside me."

Nick frowned. "Your guardian angel, you mean? You think you needed an angel to protect you from me, because I suggested you might want to end the sufferin' of some poor sick old man?"

Jim shook his head. "No, Nick," he said gently. "I *know* who you are. I'll be going now."

"You think so, do you?" Nick's voice was suddenly strong; he did not bother with further denials.

"I do, Nick. And I reckon I might have a better shot at Heaven than I thought, or you wouldn't have troubled yourself with me." He thrust out a hand to shake. "I thank you for that, Nick. A fallen angel is still an angel, and I reckon that one way or another every angel, fallen or not, is God's will made manifest."

Nick looked down at the hand, then back up at Jim's face.

And then he vanished, without taking Jim Tuckerman's hand, and he left nothing behind but the odor of brimstone.

Unicornucopia

The cycle had finally turned; I knew the Change had come at last, and magic was returning to the world.

For a thousand years and more magic had been fading, withering, dying, but now the gates of Faerie were open once more, and *mana* was spilling out into mundane reality.

This was the opportunity not merely of a lifetime, but of a dozen, a hundred lifetimes. The world had been so long without magic that the only wizards left were a few doddering old fools who had hung on past their time, a few crazies who had never realized their spells didn't work, and only a handful of scholars like myself.

All that magic, and no one who knew how to use it!

Oh, soon enough every fortune-teller and New Age loon in New York would catch on, would realize that real power could be had--but in the interim, I was free to shape the substance of reality to suit myself.

It's fortunate for all of you that I'm basically a modest, well-meaning man.

I could, I suppose, have had power over all of you. I could have summoned djinni, erected a palace of ivory and gold, enslaved whole nations, taken half of Hollywood as my harem... and to be honest, I seriously considered it.

Hey, who wouldn't?

On the other hand, I could have ended war and hunger and want, I suppose. I thought about that, too.

But it wouldn't last. I didn't want to change human nature--I was afraid I'd wind up the only true thinking person left on a planet of zombies, and I couldn't face that. And without changing human nature, how could I bring peace? Seriously, now, no idealistic propaganda--do you really think any peace would last out the day?

Magic has limits.

And if I had managed it, I wouldn't have been able to maintain it; as I said, in a few weeks, months at the most, wizards would be springing up on every side. I would have a head start, and I thought I could keep an edge, but I didn't think I was going to make it as world ruler, either benevolent or otherwise.

So I looked at other goals. I had a bit of a fling--I mentioned a harem, didn't I? And I did some traveling, and one thing and another.

But then I decided it was time to settle down. I'd been playing with time a bit, so it was still early, no one else was really aware of the magic yet, though the hints were certainly there. I went back to the university, conjured myself a pleasant little estate on the edge of town, and sat down to think out just what I wanted to do with the rest of my life.

I wanted to study, of course, and learn; I could do that, with or without magic, though the magic wouldn't hurt any.

And I wanted a home and a family.

I considered that carefully. A home I now had, and infinitely better than my old apartment it was. But a family?

I mentioned the harem, didn't I?

That was fun, but they really wouldn't do as a family. I wanted a companion, a woman I could share my life with--and I knew just the person.

Helen Pettigrew.

She and I were old friends, we'd dated a few times, but she had never taken me very seriously. A medievalist specializing in the arcane arts? An instructor without tenure? Why should she take me seriously?

I'd hoped that something might develop between us, but it never really had.

Now, though--now, things were different.

It wasn't hard to make the date. It was surprisingly easy to convince her to come see my new house, too. I was hopeful.

The expression on her face when she first stepped inside was absolutely priceless. She stared up at the chandelier, at the grand staircase, at the carpets and the statuary and all the rest of it, and her mouth hung open as if she were a kid watching her first fireworks.

"Al," she exclaimed, "how can you possibly *afford* it?"

I smiled. "Magic," I said.

"No, seriously," she said. "This place must cost a *fortune!*"

"I *am* serious," I said. "It's magic!"

She closed her mouth to stare at me.

"Really," I told her. "Come on to my workshop, and I'll show you."

I took her hand--I don't know if I'd have been quite so bold a fortnight before, but a few days in a harem can wear down one's inhibitions. At any rate, I took her by the hand and almost dragged her back to my workroom, so eager was I to show her.

"Al," she said, "I know you've always studied magic, and alchemy, and all that, but that doesn't... it isn't *real*, you know..."

"It *wasn't*," I said. "But it is *now!*"

I flung open the door and stood aside, proudly displaying my wizard's chamber.

"What a mess," she said.

I had forgotten that the place was in rather a state of disarray. "Come on," I said, leading her in.

When we reached the center of the room she pulled free, set her feet on the floor, folded her arms, and announced, "I'm in. Now, Al, what was it you wanted to show me?"

"Magic," I said. I had been prepared for this; I took my wand from the workbench and made a few passes.

I started simple, conjuring flowers, first from the air, and then growing from the floor. I summoned songbirds, made thunder and lightning, and all the while I was explaining my discovery, how I had found that magic was returning.

She looked very dubious indeed.

"It's not all tricks?" she asked, kicking at an iris.

"No," I assured her. "It's real."

"So just what all can you do?"

"Anything," I said proudly, if a bit inaccurately. "Anything at all. I conjured up this house and everything in it!"

She cocked her head to one side and stared at me.

I suppose, had I thought about it, I would have realized just how hard all this would be to accept. I had been studying magic for so long that I had forgotten how completely most people disbelieved in it.

"Anything?" she said.

I nodded.

"You mean if I ask you to conjure something up out of thin air, you can do it? Anything I ask for?"

"Anything," I agreed. "Anything at all."

"Even something that doesn't exist?"

I nodded again, but I admit my smile wasn't quite so sincere as it had been a moment before.

Magic has limits.

"Even something that's *never* existed?" she demanded.

"Probably," I said, choosing discretion. Magic *does* have limits.

"When I was a little girl," she said, "I always wanted to see a unicorn. I used to collect them, in fact--stuffed ones, and statuettes, and pictures. If this is real magic, can you conjure up a real unicorn?"

"Of course!" I said, relieved that she hadn't come up with something utterly bizarre. "What sort of a unicorn would you like?"

"Just a unicorn. A real one, with its own magic--not just a horse with a horn."

A real, magical unicorn--that was a trifle harder than I had thought at first, as I had never before conjured anything with its own personal magic. "There are several different versions of the unicorn myth," I said, stalling, while I tried to think of the best way to tackle the job.

"All right, then," she said, "you said you could do anything, right? So bring me one of each."

I had put my foot in it, no doubt about it. "This may take awhile," I admitted.

She smiled--or perhaps, though I hate to say it of the woman I intended to love, smirked. "Try," she said.

So I tried.

I had no idea how many variations of the myth might in fact exist, so I wasn't about to try conjuring each one separately. Instead, after consulting a grimoire or two, I fished out an old umbrella stand...

I should explain, perhaps, that I didn't actually furnish the entire house piece by piece; instead I worked from photographs, conjuring up duplicates of rooms that caught my fancy. Anything I didn't care for, once that was done, I threw into the workshop for use as raw materials for future spells and transformations.

One such item was a large and ugly wicker umbrella stand that had originally manifested itself in the Victorian conservatory at the back of the house.

I took this unsightly object and placed it horizontally on my workbench, gathered up a few relics and potions, and cast the enchantment Helen had requested.

Almost immediately, a whinny sounded from the umbrella stand, and the tip of a horn appeared, white and gleaming. A head appeared, then shoulders, forelegs, chest, and a moment later a unicorn stood on my workshop floor.

Just how something that size had emerged from the umbrella stand was something of a mystery, as it was very nearly the size of a full-grown horse--but then, it was magic.

Despite Helen's insistence that she wanted a real unicorn and would not be satisfied with a mere horned horse, this beast looked to me like just that--a rather small, unusually graceful white horse with a two-foot horn on its head.

Or rather, on *his* head; I had been knocked to the floor by his arrival, and found myself with a view of the creature that left no question of his sex.

The beast was rather confused by his surroundings; his eyes were wide and staring.

Helen, after the initial shock had faded somewhat, saw the animal's expression and started forward to comfort him.

He shied away, whinnying, just as the second unicorn's horn thrust out of the umbrella stand. That golden shaft pricked the first arrival's haunch, whereupon the beast panicked and charged out through the open door.

Helen watched it go, then turned quickly back to the second unicorn as it worked its way out the aperture. Golden hooves clattered out onto the floor of my workshop as the sound of breaking furniture reached us from elsewhere in the house.

The second unicorn was scarcely out of the umbrella stand when a third horn appeared; quickly, Helen stepped forward, once again intending to comfort the new arrival and lead it out of the way.

This beast did not merely shy away; it *screamed*, shrieked with rage, and thrust at Helen with that gleaming golden horn.

Fortunately, she dodged; I had not yet troubled myself to learn any healing magic.

Of course, when I breathed a sigh of relief at Helen's escape, it occurred to me that unicorn horn was supposed to have healing properties--to be, in fact, a panacea.

In some versions of the story. Others accounted it an aphrodisiac, or a nostrum against poisons, or attributed to it various other properties.

There were rather a lot of variations on the unicorn myth, I realized.

And I had just summoned one of each. I frowned.

Another aspect struck me.

"Helen," I called, "forgive me for being indelicate..."

I was interrupted by the unicorn's second lunge, and the third unicorn's escape from the umbrella stand. The workshop was becoming rather crowded, with two people and two pseudoequines sharing space with all the customary clutter.

Helen managed to dodge safely, once again; I snatched up a wand, recalled a hasty incantation I had prepared for just such an eventuality, and cast a simple spell.

A trapdoor opened beneath Helen's feet; I had a quick glimpse of her astonishment before she vanished.

The third unicorn, a black beast with a bone-white horn, was eyeing me balefully, while a fourth had worked its head out of the umbrella stand; I repeated the spell.

The drop really *was* rather disconcerting.

We arrived unhurt in the basement, atop a pile of mattresses placed there for that purpose; a good magician *always* has an escape route prepared. Above us I could hear the stamping of several hooves; I winced at the sound of some large glass object shattering.

Helen was lying spread-eagled beside me, staring blankly at the floor-joists overhead. No sign remained of the trapdoors I had temporarily created; the heavy floorboards were unbroken. Light came from a pair of simple wall-fixtures to one side.

"As I was saying," I said, "if you'll forgive me for being indelicate, unicorns--for the most part, anyway--are said to have a very decided preference for virgins. From the reactions of those two, my dear, I suspect you don't qualify."

She cast me a look I would prefer never to see again.

"Neither do I," I added hastily.

She scarcely seemed mollified by this, but at any rate she turned her attention back to the floor above us. Something large and heavy fell; a unicorn neighed loudly.

"I," she said, "am convinced. Either you've really learned magic, or we've both gone nuts."

She blinked, then added, "Or I'm dreaming."

I assured her that this was no dream.

"All right," she said, sitting up. "So I'm convinced. You can turn it off now, and send all those unicorns away."

I chewed on my lower lip as I considered the situation.

"Not from down here, I can't," I told her. "Come on."

Together we found the stairs and made our way up to the kitchen, where we discovered a unicorn eating the curtains. The creature shied and ran at the sight of us.

"Was that one we'd seen before?" Helen asked.

I shrugged. "Who knows?" I asked. "As far as I'm concerned, if you've seen one unicorn, you've seen them all."

She hit me on the arm; I suppose it was meant in fun, but it hurt, and I didn't reply.

The dining hall now held half a dozen of the mythological creatures, five white and one black; at our entrance four of them fled, one seemed indifferent, and the last lowered its horn and prepared to charge. I waved my wand in an attempt to turn the creature to stone, and, as we dove for shelter behind the armoire, made a discovery.

Ordinary spells don't work on unicorns.

I suppose, having worked out the principles of magic long since, I should have known this, but the correct application of theory to fact is not always intuitively obvious.

I saw immediately what the situation was, though, as that nasty little beast prodded at us with its horn, forcing us farther back into the corner; the unicorn was itself sufficiently magical to be immune to other magicks.

That was, to say the least, distressing.

The unicorn thrust forward again, the armoire swayed dangerously, and I used my wand again.

We missed the mattresses this time, or at any rate I did; Helen rolled down the side of the stack before landing on top of me. I knew I had just raised a fine crop of bruises, but thought no bones were broken.

We made our way up the stairs once again, moving far more cautiously this time; unicorns scattered before us, and fortunately we encountered no belligerent variants this time as we made our way back through the house.

I think we both marveled at the variety we saw. True, most were basically white horses adorned with horns--or technically, in most cases, antlers, since the supercranial shaft was usually bone-- but there were some rather astonishing others. Those that stuck to the equine form came in every color of the rainbow and a good many hues not commonly seen, in spectra or elsewhere; sizes ranged from Clydesdale-scale down to miniatures I could have put in my hip pocket. Some had wings--feathered, leathery, or even dragonfly-fashion. And there were creatures that were scarcely equine at all--many, in fact, looked more like rhinoceri.

Or is it rhinoceroses?

I had never taken much interest in the taxonomy of monocerates, and this all came as a shock to me.

Perhaps the biggest surprise came in the foyer, where two naked girls sat upon the grand staircase, chatting cheerily.

For a moment I thought perhaps some remnant of my harem had been overlooked, but neither of these two was at all familiar in detail, though one beautiful woman may often look much like another at first glance.

These two were certainly beautiful. One was a golden blonde, while the other had hair of gleaming white that spilled down the length of her seated body and pooled on the steps and floor around her. Both were young and fresh and perfect.

They looked up at the sound of our entrance.

"Hello," Helen called. "Who are you?"

They looked at one another, then stood, and I noticed that the white-haired one had a horse's tail.

"We don't know," the other one said. "Not really, anyway."

"You're unicorns, aren't you?" I asked. "You came out of the... the thing in there." I gestured toward my workshop.

The one with the tail nodded. The other, however, hesitated.

"I think," she said slowly, "that I came out of a novel, originally. But I got *here* through the cornucopia, yes."

"A novel?" Once again, a fact I should have seen sooner struck me.

Had I asked for one of each variety of, say, ape, I'd have found myself with a representative of each species of gorilla, orangutan, chimpanzee, and so forth--perhaps each subspecies, as well. I would not, however, have summoned any of Edgar Rice Burroughs' *mangani*, because those never existed.

Unicorns, however, were *entirely* fictional, and the spell would make no distinction between fictional sources. To the powers of magic, a medieval bestiary is no more real than the newest and most derivative novel--or toy, or even a scrawled manuscript by some horse-besotted schoolgirl.

Thus, I had inadvertently summoned every variety of unicorn ever imagined, from the travel reports of medieval scholars to the saccharine designs of the My Little Pony people.

The numbers would be staggering.

And what was worse, I now realized that I had no idea how to stop the spell before it was complete. Leaving Helen talking to the two girl-unicorns, I ran for my workshop.

Unicorns were spilling out the door at a gallop, little winged ones fluttering overhead; my parlor furniture had all been trampled into kindling, and the broad bay window at the front of the house was smashed out completely, leaving a gaping hole through which unicorns poured in a shining stampede.

I tried fruitlessly to fight the current for a moment, but when half a dozen horns converged on my chest I thought better of the notion.

When I made my way back up from the cellars this time I found Helen sitting on the stairs, talking earnestly with the two unicorns; a third, equine in shape but speaking in clear, bell-like tones, stood nearby, taking part in the conversation.

The steady stream of unicorns charging through the parlor continued; I could see that the fine hardwood floor had long since lost its finish, and the sharp little hooves were now digging up splinters.

What would happen, I wondered, when the floor gave out entirely?

"Helen," I said, "my dear young visitors--I think it might be a good idea to leave."

The four of them looked at me questioningly. I pointed at the flying splinters. The parlor floor was vibrating visibly, and starting to sag.

"I believe the gentleman speaks wisely," the equinoform unicorn said gravely.

The four of us exited through the front door, while the main body of unicorns continued to make use of the ruined bay window.

We were standing on the front lawn, watching, when the first police car pulled up.

"Al," Helen said, as the officers emerged from their vehicle, "do something."

"Like what?" I asked.

"Send them away."

I blinked at her in surprise.

"Why?" I asked.

"Why? Because they're going to arrest us for turning loose all these unicorns!"

"Oh, nonsense," I said, as the police marched grimly across the lawn toward us. "They can't possibly charge us with that."

They didn't, of course; they arrested us for indecent exposure, creating a public nuisance, and resisting arrest.

We had assigned the humaniform unicorns--the two arrested with us, that is; there were others--the names Cornelia and Una. It was Cornelia, the tailless blonde, who assumed equine form and exploded the roof off the squad car, freeing us.

After that we fled into the park and watched from a safe distance as chaos spread.

It was shortly before dawn when my lovely house began to collapse in upon itself; by noon nothing remained but ruins, and still unicorns were clambering from the wreckage.

By now much of the town was awash in unicorns. A few had been captured and were being ridden by grinning young women; others roamed the streets as their fancy took them. The occasional wail of an ambulance siren implied that not everyone had avoided all those very sharp horns.

The police were far too busy to worry about us.

Helen kept asking me to do something, making suggestions, and I kept stalling.

"Why can't you stop that spell?" she demanded.

I sighed. "You have a computer, don't you, Helen?"

She conceded that she did.

"Have you ever had a program start running that you didn't want to finish, but it wouldn't accept a break command?"

"A couple of times," she admitted.

"Well, this is like that. There's no way to stop the spell without doing the equivalent of rebooting the whole system, and I can't do that with just this one little wand." I tried to smile. "Don't worry," I told her. "It can't go on forever."

She was not happy. After some thought, she began asking why I didn't do anything about all the other problems--why I didn't rebuild my house, why I didn't capture the unicorns, and so on.

I was reluctant to tell anyone just why, but finally, I admitted the truth.

"You remember," I said, "that I told you magic was loose in the world once more?"

Helen nodded.

"And that I could use it to do anything I wanted?"

She nodded again.

"That was because," I said, "nobody *else* was using it. But now they are." I waved an arm at a small herd of unicorns grazing nearby. "*They* are. Unicorns are magical. And they're using up all the magic. There isn't enough left for me to do anything major. Not with just the wand."

"Oh," she said.

Eventually, we decided there was no point in watching any more; we made our way back to Helen's apartment, put some clothes on Una and Cornelia, ate a hurried meal, and settled down to watch the news.

Thousands of unicorns were not something that could be ignored, and sure enough, the story was reported, after a fashion. Theories ranged from alien invasions to Hollywood hoaxes; there was surprisingly little mention of the possibility of real, genuine, old-fashioned magic.

Three days later, finally, the spell completed its task, and the unicorns stopped appearing.

By then the free-floating magical energy available had been reduced to nothing; I could not conjure so much as a spark with my wand. Those damned unicorns had absorbed every single trace of it.

I was not happy about this, not happy at all. All my dreams of glory were reduced to ash.

Still, I had foreseen this when I first realized that my spells did not work on unicorns. I had spent the intervening time in study and careful consideration of the situation. My own library, my own tools, were buried in the rubble of my mansion, trampled into uselessness by thousands of hooves, but the university library had a few useful texts, and of course I remembered all the basic principles involved.

It seemed to me that there would be a way to resolve this, and restore my ability to work magic, while eliminating the plague of unicorns I had unleashed, the hundreds of beasts that were devouring every lawn and garden in town. If the unicorns were returned to the nothingness whence they came, the magical energy they had absorbed would be freed.

I merely needed the right spell, and not long after the appearances ceased I came upon the way of it. A certain word, a certain gesture, and then tap the unicorn with the wand...

Ah, there was the rub. Tap the unicorn with the wand. But the beasts had scattered to the four winds, flying or galloping in all directions.

I could, I suppose, have hired unicorn hunters, though there might be certain difficulties in establishing the qualifications of any volunteers. I could have waited while they traveled the world at my expense, picking off the silly creatures one by one. I would thus have gradually regained my arts--but what good would it have done?

After all, with a plague of unicorns on the evening news, even the dimmest would-be wizard must realize that magic is no longer quite as impossible as it used to be. I'd be in competition with half a hundred crazies and charlatans for every speck or spark of power.

And after the initial confusion, the creatures were giving no one any trouble; they had scattered quite thoroughly. And almost all the stories agreed that unicorns are shy, retiring beasts, rarely glimpsed by humans. Zapping them into nonexistence would scarcely be doing humanity any great favor; in fact, were I to carry out such a pogrom, I knew I would be cordially hated by entire generations of young girls.

So there was no great good to be served; the only benefit would be a partial restoration of my wizardry.

Which, I realized, I didn't need.

After all, I had already decided that I didn't particularly crave power or recognition. I had my studies, and shortly thereafter I had my family, and that was all I really wanted.

So I paid all those vanished unicorns no further heed. And I am, I am pleased to say, quite happy.

Poor Helen, however, is not. She took it into her head to study unicorns, and ignored me when I pointed out that of all the herd that had emerged from my umbrella stand, no two were alike. Nor is she qualified to capture the poor beasts, so everything must be done by proxy.

I think it's a very good thing I had the sense to let Helen go, and to marry Cornelia instead.

Best Present Ever!

Arnie Bellingham, age seven, looked at the big package sadly. He made no move toward opening it.

He had asked for it, but he had hoped Santa would somehow know he didn't really want it. Alas, it seemed Santa's magic wasn't that thorough—or perhaps Arnie had done something to annoy Santa, and this was his punishment. He didn't *think* he had been naughty, but the big man's standards were a little vague.

"Aren't you going to open it?" his mother asked.

Arnie looked up and tried to smile. "I think I'll wait until I can take it outside," he said.

"Well, okay," she said, "but after all the fuss you made about wanting it, I thought you'd at least want to take it out of the box."

"I will," Arnie assured her. "I'm... I'm *savoring* it."

She smiled, and leaned over against Arnie's Dad, nuzzling his ear. Arnie seized his opportunity, picked up the big box, and headed back to his room. Once there he set the box on his bed and stared at it.

He really didn't want a Super Mega Soaker—but Jayden Abbott, three houses up the street, did, and Jayden had been far too naughty to expect Santa to cooperate. Jayden's parents had told him flat out that they knew he was on the naughty list, and had been pretty blunt that *they* weren't about to give him any weapons, either, not even toy ones—they did seem to have some issues with their son's behavior, even though Arnie was pretty sure they didn't comprehend the true extent of Jayden's evil. When Arnie had hinted to them that Jayden had been bullying him, the Abbotts had talked about Jayden getting carried away sometimes, Jayden didn't always know his own strength, and he and Arnie would just have to work it out between themselves. They had told Jayden to behave himself, and Jayden had been apologetic and remorseful—until the instant his mother was out of sight, whereupon he had smiled hatefully at Arnie and warned him not to try *that* again, if he didn't want more of his toys broken or stolen.

His own folks had been even less help. When Arnie had told them Jayden stole his stuff, they had punished him for lying to cover up losing things without even *asking* any of the Abbotts about it. Mrs. Abbott would at least look, and if Jayden hadn't had a chance to hide whatever it was yet, Arnie got it back. Temporarily.

But Jayden never got punished, and the thefts and breakage and threats continued. Arnie couldn't even avoid Jayden; since they were the only two boys near their age in the neighborhood, their mothers *insisted* they play together. Mrs. Abbott said Arnie was a good influence on her boy, and Arnie's Mom was always worried about Arnie spending too much time alone, so they were thrown together whether they liked it or not. Which suited Jayden just fine. It meant he had someone to hit, and a source of goodies to swipe.

Arnie had learned not to ask for anything expensive for his birthday or Christmas, since Jayden would just steal it or break it, so his folks had been surprised when he asked Santa for the biggest water gun available. They never seemed to guess it was because Jayden had grabbed him from behind on Thanksgiving, when the grown-ups were all inside getting their dinners ready, and had twisted his arm almost up to his neck, and had *ordered* him to ask for it if he didn't want to get the snot beat out of him. Jayden and Arnie both knew that Arnie would never get to use it—not unless being Jayden's target counted. The best Arnie could hope for was that Jayden would fill it with water, instead of something more inventive and disgusting, before turning it on him.

Now it was Christmas morning, and the Super Mega Soaker was here, using up all Arnie's credit with Santa for the year. He sighed as he stared at the box.

The box moved.

Arnie blinked, and stared harder. Had he imagined that? He took a step closer.

The box wobbled.

It shouldn't do that, Arnie was pretty sure. He had been planning to deliver it to Jayden unopened, so that Jayden couldn't blame him if there was anything busted or missing, but now he was having second thoughts. He put a hand on the box to steady it, and felt it jerk again.

"Okay," he said to no one. "*That's* not right."

"Hello?" a squeaky voice said, from somewhere inside the box. "Is someone out there?"

Arnie felt a sudden sinking dread. Santa had messed up, and put the wrong toy in the box. This was some talking teddy bear or something, not a Super Mega Soaker at all. If Jayden didn't get his water gun, Arnie might find himself losing a few baby teeth earlier than he wanted. He grabbed the scissors off his desk and attacked the box. A moment later he pried up a flap and started to look inside.

A tiny hand reached up out of the box, and the squeaky voice said, "About time!"

Arnie stepped back, and stared as an elf climbed out of the box.

Arnie hadn't even been sure that elves really existed. Sure, he knew Santa was supposed to have a bunch of elves working for him, making toys, but Arnie wasn't stupid; he had noticed that Santa's presents arrived looking exactly like the ones in the toy stores, so he had figured that Santa bought them all from regular factories, and the elves and the workshop at the North Pole were just a story. He had thought there might be a warehouse up in

Canada or Alaska somewhere, but not a workshop at the North Pole.

But the green-clad, pointy-eared thing staring at him out of the Super Mega Soaker box was unquestionably an elf, and not a talking teddy bear.

"Hey," it said. "Where am I?"

"You're in my room," Arnie replied.

The elf looked around, taking in the Transformers bedspread and the shelves of junk. "Yeah," it said. "I can see that. But where's your room?"

"In my house," Arnie said. Then, realizing what the elf probably meant, he added, "1205 East Palmcroft Drive, Tempe, Arizona."

"Arizona?" The elf scratched his ear. "That's one of the United States, right?"

"Uh... yeah," Arnie said.

"That's all right, then," the elf said. He looked out the window. "Pretty sunny for December, isn't it?"

Arnie looked out the window as well. He shrugged. "About the same as always," he said.

The elf jumped out of the box, the bells on the curled toes of his shoes jingling, and scampered over to the window. He shaded his eyes as he looked out.

"Where's the *snow*?" he said.

"Snow?" Arnie was baffled. "It doesn't snow here."

It was the elf's turn to look baffled. "What?"

"It doesn't snow here," Arnie repeated. "Anyway, who are you, and what are you doing here? Why were you in that box?"

"I'm Dimble," the elf said, holding out a hand, which Arnie cautiously shook. "I escaped! They always told me there was no way out, that we were all trapped there for life, but I did it—I got out, and here I am!"

"Escaped from *where*?" Arnie asked, confused.

"From Santa's workshop, of course!" Dimble looked out the window again. "It *really* doesn't snow here? I'd heard there were places like that, but I thought they were a myth! If it doesn't snow, how does Santa land his sleigh?"

"I don't know," Arnie said. "I never thought about it." He hesitated, then asked, "What do you mean, escaped?"

"I got away! I'm free!"

That didn't make any sense to Arnie. "Was Santa keeping you prisoner or something?"

"Well, *duh!*" Dimble said. "Have you ever seen an elf anywhere else but the North Pole?"

"No," Arnie admitted.

"You think that's because we all *want* to stay in that frozen wasteland? Uh uh. It's because the only way in or out is in Santa's sleigh, unless you want to walk across about a thousand miles of ice and snow."

That didn't sound right at *all*. "But I thought Santa was a good guy!" Arnie protested.

"That's what they *want* you to think," Dimble said, tapping a finger on his head. "That's what they tell all of us. They say it isn't safe anywhere else, that elves were almost extinct until Santa brought our ancestors to the Pole, but I don't buy it. He just wants a supply of cheap labor, so he set up his workshop in the middle of nowhere and tells us scare stories about the rest of the world."

"You really think so?" Arnie asked.

"I'm *sure* of it!"

"But *you* got out."

"Sure, by hiding in that box," Dimble said, pointing at the empty carton. "Santa delivered me here right on schedule. But none of the others had the brains and nerve to try it."

"Wow," Arnie said.

"Yeah. I got tired of copying all the toys kids asked for, so I buried that Super Mega Soaker in a snowdrift behind the brewery, and got my buddy Kibz to seal me in the box and make sure it went on the sleigh, and here I am!"

That reminded Arnie of something. "The Super Mega Soaker?"

"Yeah."

"It's in a snowdrift at the *North Pole*?"

"Yeah." Dimble saw the horrified expression on Arnie's face, and said, "Is that a problem? I know you asked for one, kid, but I can make it up to you somehow—I'm pretty good with my hands."

"It wasn't for me," Arnie said, swallowing. "It was for Jayden, up the street. He's going to beat me up if I don't give it to him."

Dimble looked shocked. "He *what*?"

"He'll beat me up."

It was the elf's turn to look horrified. "But... but... nice kids don't *do* that!"

"He's *not* a nice kid," Arnie said. "He's a naughty one. That's why he had *me* ask for the Super Mega Soaker—Santa never brings him *anything*."

"But... but that's not *right*," Dimble said. "Good kids are supposed to get their presents to keep. Naughty kids aren't supposed to take them!"

Arnie grimaced. "Tell Jayden that."

"I will!" Dimble exclaimed. "You just wait and see, I will!" Then he hesitated. "Um... how old is this Jayden?"

"Eight," Arnie said. "And he's big for his age."

"Hey, I can take an eight year old!" Dimble said, puffing out his chest. "Just you wait and see."

Arnie looked at the elf, which stood scarcely a foot and a half tall including his green cap, and tried not to show his disbelief. Maybe Dimble knew kung fu or something, he thought.

"You show me this bully," Dimble said, "and I'll give him the thrashing he deserves!"

"Okay," Arnie said. "I'll take you over to his house this afternoon." Maybe that would take care of the problem of the missing water gun—Arnie could show Jayden the empty box and tell him there'd been a screw-up, and the elf would back up his story, even if he couldn't beat Jayden up.

Or maybe the elf really *could* beat up Jayden. Elves were magical, weren't they? Dimble had somehow survived the trip from the North Pole with no food, water, or air-holes; maybe he was stronger than he looked.

Nonetheless, Arnie was wary, a few hours later, as he approached Jayden's house, cutting across the back yards as usual. Dimble was back in the box, which was tucked under Arnie's arm. Jayden liked to surprise his visitors. He had once surprised Arnie with a whiffle bat to the head, and when Arnie protested Jayden had shrugged and said, "Hey, it's just plastic. Be glad I didn't have a wood one."

Arnie rounded the final fence cautiously, and there was Jayden, throwing a kickball up and catching it. He spotted Arnie, and said, "*There* you are!" as he flung the ball straight at Arnie's face. "What took so long? Did you get it?"

Arnie ducked, and the ball bounced off the plank fence, ricocheting harmlessly off to the side. Neither boy paid any attention to it as Jayden focused his attention on the box under Arnie's arm.

"You *did* get it!" he said. "Bring it here!"

"There's a problem," Arnie said, but then Jayden was grabbing the box and pulling it free, and Arnie decided he didn't need to say anything. Jayden would find out for himself, soon enough.

Jayden dropped the box to the ground, fell to his knees, and tore open the cardboard flaps—and a foot and a half of angry elf jumped up and socked him in the nose.

"Hey!" Jayden said, and Arnie expected him to grab at his nose—Arnie knew that that's what *he* would have done. Jayden, though, was made of sterner stuff, and instead he grabbed at Dimble's throat, closing both hands around the elf's neck.

The elf's eyes widened in surprise, and he thrust a tiny fist at Jayden's chin. It glanced off as the boy jerked his head aside.

"You wanna fight?" Jayden said. "Okay, let's fight, then!" He stood up, his hands still locked around Dimble's neck.

Dimble flailed wildly, kicking both feet at Jayden's belly, both hands jabbing at his face. Jayden did nothing to avoid these blows, beyond blinking whenever one came near his eyes.

Arnie watched, not saying a word. It was quite clear that Dimble did *not* know kung fu, or have any sort of magical fighting prowess.

Jayden let the elf pound futilely for a moment, then turned, took two long steps, and slammed the elf against the fence.

"Owww!" Dimble squealed.

Jayden swung again, and a third time, and Dimble went limp. Arnie gasped. Jayden held his captive up and looked at it.

"Holy jeez," he said. "It's an elf!"

"Yeah," Arnie said.

"Cool! Where'd you get it?"

"It was in the box instead of the gun," Arnie said.

"No foolin'? Wow." Jayden stared at the dangling creature. "That might be even better than a soaker!"

Arnie made a noise that he hoped Jayden would take as agreement.

"Here, you take it," Jayden said, handing Dimble to Arnie. "I gotta show my mom, but she says never to bring animals in the house."

"I don't think an elf is—" Arnie began, as he took the limp elf from his tormentor.

"You hold on, okay? If you let it get away I'll knock the crap outta you."

Before Arnie could reply, Jayden had turned and was running toward the house, bellowing, "Hey, Mom! You gotta see this!"

Arnie stood, and watched him go. Then he looked down at Dimble, and saw one eye open.

"Is he gone?" the elf whispered.

"Yeah," Arnie said. "But he's coming right back."

"Then let me get the heck out of here!"

"I thought you were going to thrash him."

Dimble blushed. "I guess I misjudged a little," he said.

"A little," Arnie agreed.

"Come on, kid, let me go! Nobody's supposed to know elves are still around. I can't let him keep me prisoner—if I was gonna do that, I might as well have stayed home!"

"What'll you do, though? Where will you go?"

Dimble let out a shuddering sigh. "I don't know," he said. "I guess I'll head north."

"Back to the North Pole?"

"Eventually, maybe. Come on, kid, don't let him take me!"

"He'll beat me up if I let you go."

"No, he... I... oh, heck, kid, I'm sorry, but please..."

Arnie sighed deeply. He dropped Dimble to the lawn. "Merry Christmas," he said.

"Thanks, kid—you *are* on the nice list!" Dimble tipped his hat, and then scurried away. He moved much faster than Arnie would have expected, and was long gone by the time Jayden and his mother appeared.

"Come on, Mom!" Jayden said, pulling at his mother's hand. "You gotta see the elf!"

"I'm coming. Hello, Arnie."

"Hello, Mrs. Abbott," Arnie replied.

"Where is it, Arn?" Jayden demanded.

"Where's what?" Arnie asked. Jayden wouldn't hit him with his mother right here, he knew that. As for later, Jayden was already going to kick his butt for letting Dimble go; lying about it probably wouldn't make it any worse.

Jayden stared at him. "What are you, retarded? Where's the *elf?*"

Arnie was committed now. "What elf?" he asked.

"Don't be stupid," Jayden said. "The elf. The one that was here! The one I beat up!"

"I don't know what you're talking about."

Jayden stared at him, then turned to his mother. "It was here, Mom, I swear! A real elf, with a funny hat and jingle bells on its feet!"

"Jayden, elves aren't real," Mrs. Abbott said. She sounded worried. "You're old enough to know that."

"But I saw it, Mom! One of Santa's elves! It tried to hit me, so I picked it up and knocked it around, and I gave it to Arnie to hold, and he let it get away!"

"There are no elves, Jayden. Santa isn't real. We told you that." She glanced at Arnie, her expression momentarily even more worried. She probably thought she shouldn't have said that in front of him, but it didn't bother Arnie; he'd heard grown-ups say Santa wasn't real before. He figured it was just more weird adult stuff, like all that politics talk, or the kissing thing.

"But I saw it!" Jayden insisted. "I held it in my hands! I hit it against the fence!"

She turned back to her son, her expression still worried, but now angry as well. "You did what?"

"I hit it against the fence. It was kicking me!"

She turned to Arnie. "Did you see this?"

"No, ma'am."

"Did he have an animal of some kind that he was abusing?"

"I don't know, ma'am. I didn't see one."

"Did you see an elf?"

"No, ma'am. Of course not. Elves are just baby stories."

Jayden's mouth fell open as he stared at Arnie. "You *liar!*" he said.

Arnie didn't say anything; he just tried to look innocent.

Mrs. Abbott grabbed Jayden by the arm. "I've had enough of this," she said. "We've put up with you being rude and destructive too long, because boys will be boys and we thought you'd outgrow it, but now even your *fantasies* are about hitting things! I don't care what your father says, Jayden, you are going to see a therapist, and you are going to stop telling stupid lies, and you are going to start behaving like a civilized human being. It's Christmas, and here you are making up stories about hurting *Santa's elves!*" She looked at Arnie. "Arnie, go home, please. I'm afraid Jayden is not going to play with you today."

"Okay, Mrs. Abbott."

"I think Jayden may be going to a new school soon, too."

"I'm sorry to hear that," Arnie lied.

"Run on home."

"Yes, ma'am." Arnie turned, picked up his empty box, and headed home. As he walked, he heard Jayden screaming wild protests about elves and stolen water guns and Santa cheating.

He saw no sign of Dimble. He hoped the elf was okay.

As he arrived in his own yard his mother was standing by the back door. "Oh, *there* you are!" she said. She saw the open box in his hand. "How's the squirt gun?"

"Fine," Arnie said. "I let Jayden borrow it."

She frowned. "I'm not sure that was a good idea," she said. "Oh, I found this in the wrapping." She held out a booklet.

Arnie took it, and saw it was the instructions for the Super Mega Soaker. It was sticky on the back—apparently it had been stuck to the outside of the box. "Thanks, Mom," he said. He opened it, mildly curious about the toy he hadn't gotten.

There was handwriting in it, in green ink. Startled, Arnie glanced up at his mother, but she was already walking back into the house. If she had written a note in it, Arnie thought she would have stayed around to watch him read it. He looked down at the instructions.

"Arnie—" the note said, in unfamiliar, old-fashioned handwriting that was surprisingly easy to read. "You didn't really want the Super Mega Soaker anyway, did you? And Dimble needed a chance to see the world. Hope it works out. Don't worry, I'll find Dimble and pick him up before he gets into too much trouble. Merry Christmas!" It was signed, "Santa."

Arnie stared at it, and almost tripped as he walked into the kitchen door.

"So did you like your present?" his mother asked from where she stood by the sink.

Arnie looked up at her, and broke into the biggest grin he'd worn since the Abbotts moved in up the street. He looked at the empty box, at the instructions, and at the box again.

"I loved it!" he said. "Best present ever!"

Three Days Late for the Hanging

We were three days late for the hanging, so there wouldn't be much to see, but I stopped in Osborne anyway. We needed supplies, and I thought I'd pay old Tom my respects. Dan Bates didn't have any objection—leastways, none he saw fit to communicate to me, given as he wasn't able to talk just then, so getting my attention could be a touch problematic. Oh, he'd act up right enough if he thought it was important, but a visit to Osborne didn't trouble him sufficient to stir him to action. He went where I pointed him without putting up a fuss.

Osborne wasn't that much of a town. The main street was about three blocks long before it trailed off to nothing at either end, and the two cross streets didn't go but a block in either direction before petering out. There were a few establishments outside that tight little collection of streets, but for the most part, that was what there was to see. The courthouse was dead in the center, of course, on the south side of Main Street, but they'd had the good taste to build their gallows around back, where it wouldn't trouble any townsfolk who might be of a sensitive nature. I thought I should go take a look.

Not that I saw any townsfolk about, just now, but then it was a mighty hot afternoon.

I didn't need to use my heels on Dan, just pointed him in the right direction, and he ambled around the courthouse to the square.

There was the scaffold, fresh-built of raw lumber by the look of it, and there was old Tom, dangling from the crossbeam. That was a bit of a surprise, that they hadn't taken him down and buried him, the climate being what it was, but it was an even bigger surprise when Tom kicked up his foot at me.

I frowned, and hopped down off Dan's back. I could see now that Tom was watching me, and moving his tongue as if he were trying to talk, but he couldn't get a word out with that noose around his neck. Didn't have the air. And he couldn't wave or sign to me, as his hands were tied behind his back.

I walked over to the base of the scaffold and looked up at him and said, "You ain't dead."

I could read in his expression that he was well aware of that fact, and didn't much appreciate my pointing it out as I had.

"Seems to me that must mean Seth Pemberton ain't dead, neither."

It's a sorry thing to see a man with his neck in a noose try to nod.

"Well, why the hell *not?* Seems to me that was at the heart of our agreement, Tom—you were to kill that son of a bitch." My frown got a tad deeper. "And if you didn't kill him, what the dickens are they hangin' you for?"

"Horse theft," someone said, and I turned to find a young fellow with a shiny badge standing behind me.

"Howdy," he said. "Sounds to me as if you know a few things about old Tom, here."

"A few," I said. I held out my hand. "I'm called Nick Blaisdell."

We shook. "Al Perkins," he told me. "Deputy sheriff."

"Saw the badge," I said, nodding. "You the one that hanged him?"

"Nope," he said. "I'm just the one they've got watching him." He jerked his head toward the gallows.

I glanced at Dan, who was watching all this, but he didn't do anything to express his opinion on the situation. Then I turned back to the deputy. "Seems to me," I ventured, "that it's traditional that if a man survives hangin', he gets a reprieve."

"We ain't particularly set on tradition here in Osborne," he said. "The judge sentenced him to be hanged by the neck until dead, so that's what we're doing. If the rope had broke, or his neck hadn't, maybe we'd reconsider, but as it is, we're plannin' to abide by the sentence as handed down."

"So he's been there three days?"

"He has."

"Seems a mite unnatural, wouldn't you say?"

"Brother, I won't lie to you, this is the most unnatural thing I've ever heard tell of outside a storybook, and it's got us all fair disturbed, but what are we to do, but wait?"

I could see his position, though it wasn't the sort of thinking I'd have expected. It made matters a trifle awkward. I knew that he wasn't going to die no matter how long they kept him dangling there, so long as Seth Pemberton was still alive, and Pemberton was a healthy young fellow who might have forty or fifty years left before he came to the end of his natural span.

Of course, he was also a bloody-handed bastard who might get shot down any day, and none would say he didn't have it coming, but that wasn't anything a man could count on. Divine justice generally seemed to be reserved for the next life, not this one, and many a wicked sinner lived to a ripe old age and died rich and happy in bed. Leaving old Tom hanging there until Seth Pemberton expired could be more than a little troublesome for all concerned, myself included.

"What do you reckon it's about?" I asked.

The deputy shook his head. "Can't say I know."

"But after three days, *somebody* must have come up with an explanation!"

"Oh, dozens of them! But we've no way to tell which might be true."

"Couldn't you ask Tom? I know he can't talk, but he could kick right for yes, left for no."

"We tried that. Don't rightly think I believed him."

"What's he say, then?"

"Says he made a deal with the Devil."

I tried not to sigh. I hated the way my customers insisted on assuming I was the Devil, no matter how often I denied it. "What, says he sold his soul for eternal life? How's *that* work?"

"Not for eternal life. But we couldn't make out what he claims he got. Whatever it was, the preacher who was askin' the questions reckons Tom didn't carry out his end of the deal, and can't die till he does."

"Well, if that's the case, then it seems right cruel to keep him hanging there, where he can't possibly make good on his bargain."

Tom commenced to kicking when he heard that, but the deputy didn't pay him any mind. Dan cocked his ear, but that was all.

"We thought about that," Deputy Perkins said. "And there's something to it—but then again, if that's the truth, why would we want to help him conduct the Devil's business?"

These people were putting far too much logical thought into this. I was more accustomed to folks who were too scared to think straight when they saw something like Tom's hanging. Most folks would do whatever it took to make the strangeness go away, without worrying about whether it suited some cosmic authority.

"'Sides," Mr. Perkins continued, "I don't believe Lucifer goes about this world making deals with the likes of Tom Cutler." He tipped his head. "Leastways, I didn't until maybe ten minutes ago."

I didn't like the sound of that one bit. "How's that?" I asked.

"As I was coming back just now I heard you saying something about an agreement you had with old Tom."

That's just what I had feared. "Did you?"

"I did. And something about killing a Seth Pemberton."

This fellow had some mighty fine hearing, he did. That was more than a bit unfortunate, from my point of view. "That so?"

It was the deputy who sighed this time. "Mister," he said, "I ain't fool enough to pull a gun on the Devil himself, and if you ain't him I've got no good *reason* to pull a gun on you, but I think you'd better start explaining just who you are and why you're here."

"I believe I told you I'm called Nick Blaisdell."

"Didn't ask what you were *called*," he retorted.

"Deputy, do you really think the Devil would come riding in here on a mule, wearing a dirty old Stetson and boots with the heels worn down? I'd heard Old Scratch was a snappy dresser."

Dan gave me a dirty look and made a sort of whinny; he never cared to be called a mule, and never mind that to all accounts and purposes he happened to be one just then.

The deputy didn't pay Dan any mind. "If you ain't the Devil, then what's this agreement you were discussing with old Tom?" he asked.

"I didn't say I wasn't what you might call a conjure man," I told him. Of course, I didn't say I *was*, either, but I didn't tell him that. "I did make a bargain with Tom Cutler, and I reckon it's why he's still breathing."

"He *ain't* breathing. That's what's so...well, he ain't breathin'. But he ain't dead, either."

"Fine, then—why he ain't dead."

"Go on."

"Mr. Cutler had a bit of trouble with a Mr. Seth Pemberton," I said. "*Bad* trouble, if the truth be told. He was of a mind that Mr. Pemberton had done him a great wrong, but he couldn't prove it enough for a court of law, and he wasn't no sort of a gunman, where Mr. Pemberton has a reputation as a mean fellow and a dead shot. So Tom and me, we were drinking together in a saloon out by Black Hawk, and he told me his situation, and I said I could make certain he could kill Seth Pemberton, and Pemberton wouldn't lay a hand on him to stop him."

"How'd you fix to do that?"

"I have a certain few talents, you might say. I can't exactly stop the hand of Death, but I can arrange terms with the Grim Reaper, after a fashion, and I did. I made it so that Death won't touch Tom Cutler until after Seth Pemberton's gone to meet his maker. What's more, to make sure old Tom had a good shot, I made it so that Pemberton can't see him no how, not ten feet away in broad daylight."

"Then what?"

"Then I went about my business, and left old Tom to his, which I *thought* included dispatching Seth Pemberton."

"If you felt obliged to help out Tom Cutler, why didn't you just kill this Pemberton yourself?"

I shook my head. "Can't do it, Deputy. I may have powers beyond those of ordinary men, but just so, I'm bound by laws beyond those that bind you. I can't kill a man by my own hand— nor a woman, nor a child. Even if a judge decided it wasn't murder, it'd be the end of me." I gestured at poor Tom. "I can't break any number of laws. I can't even creep back here by night and cut him down without the say-so of the judge."

Perkins chewed on that for a moment. "Don't know as I believe that," he said at last. "Don't know as I believe a thing you say, come down to it. If it weren't for old Tom there, I'd think you were some kind of confidence man, spinning a yarn to trick me into something."

I spread my hands. "Can't see as how I can convince you, then. I'm not lying, but my saying that don't make it so, and if you think I'm lying then nothing I say is going to change your mind."

"Wouldn't go *that* far. But I'm not gonna take your every word as gospel, either. You've got the best explanation I've heard yet as to why old Tom ain't dead, but I'm not ready to put money on it— nor anything *more* than money."

"I don't want your soul, Deputy. Devil or swindler or conjurer, whatever I may be, you have my word on that."

"I'm pleased to hear it, but that don't really help with the situation we have here." He turned to Tom, who had been watching us. "You heard what he's been saying?"

Tom did the jerk of his head that was as close to a nod as he could manage.

"He tellin' the truth?"

There was the jerk again.

"Kick your right leg for yes, the left for no."

Tom kicked his right leg.

The deputy stood there, contemplating Tom, and I decided to sum up where we found ourselves. "Well, here's the way of it, so far as I can see," I said. "Old Tom Cutler's going to hang there alive until either he's cut down, or Seth Pemberton dies. I can't rightly kill Pemberton, not any way I can imagine, and I can't cut Tom down, so I'm out of the matter 'cept for offering a little advice if anyone cares to listen. You don't choose to believe me, that's your right—it's a free country, they tell me. I'll be on about my business if that's the case, once I've said my farewells and apologies to poor Tom, and you can do as you please. I'll tell you, though, that he ain't gonna die until Pemberton does, and it'd be a right shame if Mr. Pemberton don't come to a bad end pretty soon."

"You can't take your spell off him?"

"'Tain't a spell, and no, I can't. Once I make a bargain I can't change the terms, and especially when death's involved." A thought struck me, a bit off the path we'd been following. "You said he was hanged for horse theft? How sure are you he done it?"

"Pretty damn sure. Seems he had a bad night at cards, got drunk in the process, then lit out on Bill Barrett's chestnut mare in front of a dozen witnesses who warn't as drunk as he'd thought they might be. Barrett offered a half-eagle to any man who brought the son of a bitch back, and Jack Brown took him up on it. Jack can ride better 'n any man I ever saw, black or white, and has this big bay stallion... well, Barrett's mare wasn't gonna outrun him."

I nodded. I knew old Tom had no sense when he'd been drinking; I'd seen that in Black Hawk. "Seems plain enough. Surprised he didn't claim extenuating circumstances and get it reduced to a stay in jail, though."

Deputy Perkins shook his head. "Our Mr. Cutler's done a mighty fine job of aggravatin' every man and woman in Osborne over the years, and he damn near knocked out Jack Brown's front tooth before he went down, so wasn't a soul in town believed he hadn't known what he done."

I hadn't apprehended that Tom was quite so unpopular as that. I'd seen from the first, the day we met, that he was bound for the gallows, and even when and where it would happen, which was why I'd been willing to deal with him, but I'd thought he'd have done in Seth Pemberton by then, and get hanged for *that*. It didn't sound as if any pleas for mercy would do a lick of good. I turned to Tom and called, "What the hell were you *doin'*, this past four months, that you didn't get around to killin' Pemberton?"

Tom kicked, but couldn't give me an answer.

This was a hell of a mess. It wasn't going to do me or mine a lick of good having Tom hanging there, unable to die, but I couldn't do a thing by my own hand. I'd said I wasn't going to do anything but make my goodbyes, but I couldn't go without trying to talk out a solution.

For one thing, I'd promised Tom that he'd have a chance to kill Seth Pemberton, and my word's good. I can't break a promise, any more than I can break a law. Some might say as I gave him a chance and he didn't take it; I'd promised he *could* kill Pemberton, not that he *would*. I might not have a choice but to say that myself, but it sailed a little closer to the wind than I wanted to explain if certain powers were to ask me about it. I wanted shut of the whole business, as soon as it could be arranged.

"Listen, Deputy," I said. "I got no right to ask you, and you already said you don't trust me, and there ain't no reason you should, but let me make a suggestion. You say no, that's an end to it, and I'll be on my way, but I hope you'll give it some thought."

"I'm listenin'."

"What if you were to cut old Tom down, and let me take him down to Rawlinsburg, where Seth Pemberton's got a place? Then when matters there are settled, I'll bring the body back here so the judge can see the sentence has been carried out, and he'll go to the undertaker, and we won't need to say no more about the delay."

"The body? You mean Pemberton's?"

"No, I mean old Tom's. What would the judge want with Pemberton?"

"You think he'll die?"

"Once Pemberton's dead? I surely do."

"But why should he, once he's free of the noose?"

"You said his neck's broke, didn't you?"

The Deputy's mouth came open, then closed again. He frowned. "But you're askin' me to countenance settin' him free to commit a murder."

"And he's already been hanged, so he ain't gonna get away with it."

I could see Perkins wrestling with that. "We didn't hang him for murder."

"Does it matter?"

He considered that, then said, "Maybe it don't. But you're asking me to let him go kill someone. Ain't no judge sentenced this Pemberton to die."

"I see how that's a stickin' point, Deputy, but I give you my word, if there was ever a man the law couldn't touch who deserves to die, it's Seth Pemberton."

Perkins chewed his lip for a moment, then said, "It'd be more than my job is worth if I cut him down, and what's more, I don't know if he's fit to take on this Mr. Pemberton. I'm pretty sure his neck *did* break, and it might be that once he's out of that noose and don't have the rope holdin' things in place, he won't be able to move a muscle. Not to mention, he's all swole up. Just because he's still alive don't mean he's in any shape to kill a man. Which brings me to another point. If he kills this Pemberton, then he's gonna die himself, is that right?"

I nodded.

"Then why in God's name would he *want* to kill Pemberton? It'd be suicide!"

I opened my mouth to say something about how old Tom was mad for vengeance, and how he must be suffering the torments of Hell with his neck broke and all, but then I stopped. A man's life can be agony, but he'll still fight to keep it. Oh, not every man, but some, and I wouldn't put it past Tom to be one of them. Besides, he'd had four months, and hadn't gone after Pemberton; why would he do it now, when he wouldn't before? Instead of speaking I closed my mouth and pursed my lips all thoughtful.

"Now, I shouldn't be sayin' this, bein' a lawman and all," Perkins continued, "but you say *you* can't kill this Pemberton, and *I* don't know him and ain't got no business looking for trouble out his way, and Tom, there, we can't trust to kill Pemberton no matter what he says, even if he's got the strength to do it after bein' up there all this time, but you say there's scarce a soul who knows him who don't think Pemberton needs killin'. So why don't you go see if you can maybe find someone *else* who'll do him in, and put Tom out of his misery?"

I drew in a breath, but before I could speak Dan Bates let out a loud bray.

"Hush, you fool brute," I said. Then I turned back to Perkins. "Deputy, I told you I can't break the law against killin', and that means I can't go about askin' someone to commit murder. Tom, there, said he'd kill Pemberton if he had a chance, so I didn't have to ask, but findin' some other fellow and suggesting he take a shot, that'd be inciting, or aiding and abetting, or some such, wouldn't it?"

"Might be," he admitted.

"I'd need to find someone who'd do it without me askin'. Now, maybe if I tell them about poor Tom and get up some sympathy, the thought will come to someone's mind..."

Dan brayed again, long and loud.

"*Hush*, I said..." Then I stopped.

"Oh," I said. "You volunteering?"

Perkins started. "Me? Now, what did I say to give you *that* idea? I told you it ain't my business."

"No, not you, Deputy. Never mind. Just... I may have a way to put an end to poor Tom's suffering."

"I'd be pleased to hear about it."

"Maybe you would, but I ain't gonna tell you. I'm sorry, Deputy, but it's best you not be involved." I tipped my hat. "My thanks for speaking to me, and setting my mind straight, but I'll be going now. Got a long ride ahead."

He stared at me for a moment, then shrugged. "I'd be obliged, Mr. Blaisdell, if you didn't come back this way."

"I can't promise, but I'm hopin' I won't have any call to." Then I let Dan have his head, and he turned and began walking back out of the square, a little faster than his usual pace. I didn't wave to Tom; didn't seem the kindly thing to do.

When I was sure we were out of earshot, out of Osborne entirely and back in the open, I leaned forward and said to my mount, "So *you're* volunteering to kill Seth Pemberton?"

Dan nodded vigorously.

"And you're thinking this'll pay off the rest of your debt?"

He nodded again.

"I can see how that would be fair enough," I acknowledged. "But you know you'll have to do it the way you are now, don't you? Because if I turn you back to a man, I'd be assisting in a murder. If a mule kills Pemberton, *that* ain't murder. Still want to try?"

That third nod was slow in coming and wasn't half as big, but come it did, in good time.

"Well," I said, sitting back upright. "I'd say that's fair enough and the best for all concerned 'cept Mr. Pemberton. You settle this matter, and you're quit with me; the moment it's done you'll be a man again, and not a mule."

He let out a bray I took to mean he was pleased to hear it.

"Seems to me," I told him, "that we owe it to old Tom to get to Rawlinsburg quick as we can, then, don't we?"

And with that, he picked up his feet more briskly than ever I'd seen him do before, and we set out down the southwest road.

Took us close to a week to get to Rawlinsburg, which had me feeling bad for poor old Tom, but there wasn't a faster route I knew, and the weather didn't cooperate, and no matter how eager he was to shed that mule skin and be a man again Dan Bates couldn't keep up his top speed through a downpour and across mudslides and flooded gullies. The rain did stop eventually, around the fourth day, and we got there in the end, both of us on foot by then because I thought Dan had done enough to earn a break.

Rawlinsburg was maybe twice the size of Osborne, I'd say. Wasn't a mining town in the strict sense, in that there wasn't a mine in it, but there were half a dozen in the surrounding hills, and Rawlinsburg was where the miners came to drink up their profits, or drown their sorrows when there weren't profits to be had. The assay office and the bank were near the center of town, one of each, and there were two general stores, across the street from each other, but there were four big saloons, one at each corner where Main Street crossed Broadway.

Mr. Seth Pemberton had himself a place a mile or so northwest of town, and had a hand in at least two of the four saloons, though it wasn't clear whether he so much owned a piece of them or just collected a share of their earnings out of the generosity of the folks that operated them. There'd been a time when he played cards at the Silver Nugget most every evening, but wasn't a man in town would play against him any more, though none would say outright that he cheated. Wasn't anyone who'd say he started out as a claim-jumper, neither, at least not if they thought it might get back to him. You might hear tell that he treated the women at the cathouses rough, though, because he didn't mind that people knew that; hell, he took pride in it.

I surely did wonder sometimes why no one had shot him. Yes, he was a dead shot, but ain't no matter how good a man is if he's ambushed and shot in the back. Still, it hadn't happened yet.

I'd gone over all of this with Dan on the road from Osborne, though he'd known some of it before; he'd been with me about two years, all in all, so he'd heard me talking to old Tom Cutler some when we made our agreement, even if he hadn't been allowed in the saloon where we were drinking. Mules do have those big ears, after all, and they ain't just for looks.

We walked into town and headed for the Silver Nugget, and after the journey we'd had I felt sorry that I couldn't take Dan in with me and give him a shot of whiskey. I tied him to the rail where he could reach the horse trough, then went inside.

I could surely get *myself* a shot of whiskey, which I did, and despite it being the worst sort of rotgut I followed it up with two more. With that taken care of, I asked the saloonkeeper where Seth Pemberton might be found—in town, or at home?

"In jail," he told me.

That came as an unpleasant surprise—a surprise because I'd had the impression that Mr. Pemberton had the townsfolk of Rawlinsburg sufficiently cowed that he could pretty much do as he pleased without consequences, and unpleasant because it would be awkward to get a mule into a cell. But on the other hand, if Pemberton were to be hanged that would solve everyone's problems except perhaps Dan Bates', as he would need to find another way to earn back his humanity.

"Why?" I asked, hoping it was for murder—or horse theft, which would be downright amusing.

"Drunk and disorderly. Passed out on the floor just there behind you last night, and we carried him to the jail to sleep it off."

That was a disappointment. "So he won't be *staying* there, then."

"He usually doesn't, no, but I've heard tell that someone may have filed a complaint that could hold him up a piece."

I frowned. I decided I'd have to see for myself, though I couldn't safely get any more involved than I already was. "Could you direct me to the jail?" I asked, as I put two bits on the bar.

"Just down Main Street, past the bank." He pointed in the general direction, and I tipped my hat and took my leave.

I explained the situation to Dan as I untied him and led him up the street, and he made a rude noise to express his opinion of the situation.

The jail was just past the bank, and as they both had bars in the windows I wasn't too sure I'd found it until I saw the sign over the door. I left Dan out front—didn't bother tying him this time—and pushed open the door. It was locked, but I didn't worry myself about that; if there was a law against opening a lock without a key I didn't know about it, so it didn't apply to me, and the lock itself didn't care to stop me.

Didn't seem as if Rawlinsburg had put any sort of sheriff or constabulary in charge of the jail, as there wasn't any sort of office, just a little hallway down the middle with two cells on each side and a wooden chair at the far end. A fellow with a badge on his chest and a rifle on his knee was sound asleep in the chair, and Seth Pemberton was sitting on the bunk in the far right-hand cell, slumped against the wall with his nose in the air, his eyes closed, and his mouth wide open.

"Howdy," I said.

The man in the chair didn't stir, but Pemberton gave a snort and sat up. He turned and looked at me out of bloodshot eyes, and I don't care to ever have a man look at me like that again.

"Who the hell are *you*?" he asked.

"I'm called Nick Blaisdell," I said. "I take you to be Mr. Seth Pemberton."

He didn't say whether or not I had it right; instead he got to his feet and tried the door of his cell, but it was locked, and he didn't have my knack with locks. He slammed his hand against the bars, then shouted, "Hey, Deputy! Wake up!"

The man with the rifle started, and sat up. He blinked at me, then turned to his prisoner. "What is it?" he asked.

"You gonna let me out of here?"

The deputy, if that's really who he was, started to say something to Pemberton, then looked at me instead and said, "Who're you? Did Judge Blaine send you?"

"Nope," I said. "No one sent me."

He frowned, then turned back to his prisoner and shook his head. "I'm sorry, Mr. Pemberton, but I got orders not to let you out until Judge Blaine says it's okay."

"Why the hell not? What's the judge got to do with it? I thought I was just here to sleep it off!"

"I don't know the details, Mr. Pemberton, but word is that some woman from Icy Creek came into town this morning and swore out a complaint against you for robbery and criminal assault."

Pemberton's expression changed; I wouldn't go so far as to say he looked worried, but he sure wasn't a happy man. "Icy Creek? She give a name?"

"Not one I've heard, Mr. Pemberton."

I was listening, and I was thinking. If this "criminal assault" was bad enough it might get Pemberton hanged after all, which would do for poor old Tom—or it might just let this Judge Blaine pocket a fat fine that no one would be so crude as to call a bribe, as had been known to happen before when someone tried to point a finger at Pemberton. As the people pointing the fingers tended to not live very much longer, that didn't happen too often, so hearing that this woman from Icy Creek had spoken up meant this might be a more serious matter than most.

I was so busy mulling that over that I almost didn't hear when Pemberton called, "You, Blaisdell or whatever you said your name was—you have anything to do with this?"

"Not a thing, Mr. Pemberton," I said. "I just came to find you on behalf of a fellow by the name of Cutler."

Pemberton let out a bark of laughter. "Cutler? Old *Tom* Cutler? I heard he's been hanged, over in Osborne; I don't suppose it'll do him any good that you've found me."

"That's as may be," I admitted.

Pemberton seemed to decide from that I was of no consequence. He ignored me and turned back to the deputy. "Listen, if you were to let me out of this cell, I could make it worth your while."

"Can't see my way clear to do that, Mr. Pemberton. I'm mighty sorry."

"No, you don't understand. C'mere, and I'll tell you why it'd be to your benefit."

"I can hear just fine from here, Mr. Pemberton."

"No, you'll want this to stay private, just between the two of us." He nodded his head in my direction. "Let me whisper it to you."

Now, I'm no fool, and I had a pretty fair idea what was coming, but I decided that it wasn't in my interest to interfere; I stood by the door of the jail and watched without saying a thing as that deputy came over to hear what it was Pemberton wanted to say.

I'm no fool, but I can't say the same for the deputy. Maybe he misjudged Pemberton's reach, or maybe he just didn't have the brains of a sparrow, but he stepped up close to the bars, and of course Pemberton grabbed the rifle out of his hands and pulled it into the cell. He checked to see that it was loaded, then pointed it at the deputy, who was only just then noticing it was gone.

"Unlock the cell," he said.

"Oh, come on, Mr. Pemberton..."

Pemberton raised the barrel so that it was aimed right between the deputy's eyes.

"Open the goddamned cell!"

The deputy looked at me; I shrugged. "Not my place to get involved here, Mister."

"You working with Pemberton? Sent here to distract me? Is that the way of it?"

"No, sir, I am not. I'm just staying out of it."

"Smart man," Pemberton said. "Last time I'm gonna ask, Deputy—open the damned door!" He closed his finger on the rifle's trigger.

For a moment I thought the deputy might decide to play the hero and get himself shot, but then he sighed and fetched the key and unlocked the cell door. He stood aside, hands in the air, while Pemberton emerged into the passage between cells, and I reached back and opened the door to the street. I stepped back, out of Pemberton's way.

"I *said* you were smart," Pemberton said, smiling in the nastiest way imaginable, as he hurried out with the rifle still in his hand. He wasn't running, not quite, but he was moving too fast to call it a stroll.

I turned to look out into the street after him. As I figured might happen, he saw Dan Bates standing there, not even tethered, and ran up and swung himself into the saddle. Dan responded with about the most surprised look I'd ever seen on a mule's face, staring right at me

"That's my mount, Mr. Pemberton," I called. "And horse theft's a hangin' offense."

"This ain't no horse," he shouted back. "It's a damned mule!" Then he dug in his heels and shouted, "Gee-yaw!"

Dan set off at a goodly pace, though still well short of a gallop—in all the time he'd been a mule he'd never got the hang of galloping, as it's not something a mule gets called on to do as a regular thing. I stood for a moment and watched as Seth Pemberton rode off toward the hills to the north; then I set out to follow at a leisurely pace. I didn't have any intention of catching up for a time; I was leaving this up to Dan.

Meanwhile the deputy came boiling out of the jail behind me, shouting his fool head off. He saw where Pemberton was headed, and then hurried to the nearest saloon, calling out that he wanted men for a posse.

I strolled on, paying him no mind.

Not long after that his posse, half a dozen men on horseback, came charging past me. I tipped my hat to them, but didn't say a word.

I can't rightly say *how* I knew where to stop, but being as I am, I knew, just as I'd known when and where old Tom would hang. Half a mile out of Rawlinsburg I stepped over to the roadside and sat down on a boulder to wait.

Wasn't but ten minutes later that Dan Bates, on two legs again rather than four, came climbing up from the gully on the other side of the road. He was wearing Seth Pemberton's boots, belt, and trousers, and nothing else; he had his saddle and harness slung on his broad shoulders, and was dragging my pack, which served to weigh him down some.

"No shirt?" I asked.

"Too much blood on it, and too small for me anyway," he answered cheerfully. "Gettin' into these pants was bad enough." He tossed the pack onto the road, then swung the saddle around and held it out. "This is yours."

"It is," I agreed. "Reckon I'll want to find someone else to wear it."

"You could buy yourself a *real* mule, you know."

"I could," I acknowledged, "but there's usually some idjit out there who's earned a spell on hooves, and they're usually at least a little smarter and more cooperative than mules that were *born* mules." I hefted the pack onto my shoulder, then took the saddle and harness, and patted Dan on the back. "Pemberton give you any trouble?"

"Not to speak of. He wasn't much of a horseman. Wasn't hard to throw him, once we were out of sight of town, and iron-shod hooves do a pretty good job at putting a man down." He laughed, and held out a hand. "Them shoes came right off when I changed back, but look at that middle fingernail—it's shrunk up, but you can still see a ring of nail-holes there."

I'd seen the like before, so I just nodded. "Let's get you back to town. You'll be wanting a job and a bed."

"You bet I will."

We turned our steps back toward Rawlinsburg, me carrying the saddle and pack; I figured Dan had carried them long enough that I should take a turn.

"It occurs to me," Dan said, after we had walked a little, "that you turned me back to a man as a reward for killin' two men."

"You could look at it that way," I said. "Though there are some would say that you did old Tom Cutler a mercy, and it was the rope that killed him—assuming he's genuinely dead now. I'll want to stop by Osborne and make sure of that."

He nodded. "Still, it was killin' Pemberton that put me back on two feet—the moment he stopped moving, I started changing. Seems as if there's somethin' wrong with the morality of that."

"I wasn't too concerned with the right or wrong of it," I said. "I just wanted to clean up a mess I'd made, and you helped me do that, so I owed you. And believe me, Pemberton had it coming."

"If I didn't know better, Mr. Blaisdell, I might almost think you really *are* the Devil, and by making me a murderer you've staked a claim on my soul."

"I'm not any sort of devil," I said.

"So you've always said, but after more'n two years in your company I haven't figured out what *else* you could be."

"I'm just a fellow with certain special talents, and a good working relationship with the Grim Reaper. I've got no claim on your soul, and now that you've served your term I've got no claim on any other part of you, neither. You were a good mule, but that's done. If we ever meet again after this, I hope it'll be as friends, but if you hold a grudge I can't say I'd blame you."

He shook his head. "You treated me fair enough."

I was pleased to hear him say that.

At the Rawlinsburg hotel I vouched for Dan as a trustworthy fellow who'd fallen in bad company, to explain his lack of hat, shirt, or luggage, and I put down a gold eagle to cover his expenses as what you might call a bonus for two years of good service.

When the posse came back, a little after sundown, I reported that I'd seen Seth Pemberton lying dead in a ditch, and my mule had run off. I told them where they might find the body, and asked them to let me know if anyone saw my mount.

I didn't find me anyone in Rawlinsburg who would serve as a suitable mule, so two days later I bought a horse, and despite Deputy Perkins' request I stay clear I headed back to Osborne, just to be sure.

Sure enough, I saw that old Tom was properly dead and buried, and I stopped by his grave to offer my respects. Deputy Perkins spotted me, and didn't say a word. He just watched me until he saw me ride out of town.

From there I headed up into the mountains, as I had another customer to check on in one of the mining camps out that way. I wanted to make sure this one hadn't managed to make a mess of things the way Tom Cutler had.

And of course, I was keeping my eye out for a potential mule.

The Girl Who Couldn't Fly

I was walking up the road from Baker's Corner the first time I saw her. She was sitting on a fence at the edge of town with a couple of other kids, all of them talking intently about something that was obviously very important to them, but which I suspected wouldn't matter much to adults. I reckoned she was maybe ten or eleven. At the first I didn't realize she had wings; I thought she was wearing some kind of fancy dress coat, or maybe a seriously overblown hair ornament.

But then I got a better look, and saw what was there, and I stopped and went over to say hello.

I didn't have a good reason, really; I was just curious. I'd never seen a girl with wings up close before. I'd heard about a few, but never met any.

When the kids saw me coming they all stopped talking and watched me warily.

"Hey," I said. "Is this Damonsburg?"

"Sure is, mister," said the one boy in the trio.

"Thanks. Say, are those wings?"

The winged girl shrank back and hunched down a little, and her two friends sat up straighter.

"What's it to you, mister?" the boy demanded.

I held up my hands. "Nothing, nothing! I didn't mean any harm; I just never saw anyone with wings close up before."

"Well, now you have," the boy said.

"How big are they? Could I have a look?"

The other two looked at their friend, who still didn't say a word; she looked from side to side, then leaned a little forward and spread her wings.

I should explain that you may be thinking of blonde angels with shining white wings, or black-haired beauties with wings like bats, but this wasn't either of those; she was a plain little girl with drab brown hair, and when the wings were folded down they were that same dull brown color, but feathers, not hair. I wasn't expecting much of a display.

But then they unfolded, and kept spreading until they must have been about twelve feet across from wingtip to wingtip, maybe more, and they swept up in a graceful curve, and the underside wasn't dull brown, but red and gold feathers, patterned and barred, bright and beautiful as anything you can imagine. I stopped breathing, just looking at them, at those colors shimmering in the afternoon sun.

Her friends turned to look at her wings, but didn't say anything. They didn't look as impressed as I was, but I suppose they'd seen them before.

"Lovely," I said at last.

The girl folded them down on her back again and watched me suspiciously.

"Can you fly?" I asked her.

She said, "No." It was the first time I had heard her voice, which was soft and sweet, but she sounded a little annoyed. I knew she must have heard that question a thousand times.

"Pity," I said. "But they're beautiful wings, all the same."

"They get in the way," she said. "Momma has to make special clothes for me."

"Don't you have somewhere else to go, mister?" the other girl asked, a little belligerently.

"'Course," I said. I tipped my hat. "Thanks for letting me see your wings, Miss." Then I turned and walked on into Damonsburg.

I didn't really have any business there, but then, I didn't have any business much of anywhere just then. I'd been on my own for about three years at that point, just roaming about, seeing the world and trying to decide what to do with my life, since I couldn't go home. I'd seen the witches in Abbot's Creek, and the dogs of the Salt Coast, but I hadn't yet seen anywhere I'd want to stay for more than a few months. I'd heard Damonsburg was a nice place, so I'd come to see for myself.

Those kids hadn't seemed particularly friendly, but then, practically the first thing I'd said was a nosy question about something that was none of my concern, so I didn't hold it against them.

I wondered a bit about why she couldn't fly, though; those splendid wings certainly looked big enough. Maybe she didn't have the muscles to work them properly? Maybe they weren't as aerodynamic as they looked?

But it wasn't my business.

I walked into Damonsburg and looked it over, liking what I saw; it was clean, green, and pretty, and of a reasonable size, probably about a thousand people. I wandered into a saloon that faced on the town square and read the board above the bar. They listed a dozen sandwiches, a dozen beers, and a dozen currencies they accepted, and one of the currencies was the Black God's silver, which I had some of in my pocket, so I got myself a ham sandwich and a glass of porter and settled on a stool at the bar. I asked the bartender a few questions about the town, and he answered them in a friendly fashion until I said, "I saw a girl with wings on my way into town."

His smile got a little less friendly. "That'll be Nina Parmenter. You'd do well to leave her alone. Poor kid's had enough trouble."

"I don't mean any harm," I said. "I was just curious. Never saw anyone with wings before."

He softened a bit. "I don't suppose they're common," he admitted. "You know, they wouldn't *ever* be common in any case, but they wouldn't be as rare as all that, except a lot of parents cut the wings off as soon as the baby's born."

I put my drink down and stared at him. "Now, why in the world would anyone do *that*?" I asked.

He seemed surprised by the question. "Where are you *from*?" he asked.

"Nowhere near here," I said. "What's this about chopping the wings off babies?"

"Well, stop and think about it," he said. "A kid with wings eats a lot more than a regular kid, and can't wear regular clothes, and if she gets squirmy when you're holding her you can get a feather in the eye and it can really hurt. Babies are enough work and enough trouble without putting wings on 'em."

"But...but the wings make them *special*."

"And how is that a good thing for the parents? Or for the baby, for that matter? You're setting the poor kid up to be teased for the rest of her life. Around here we've seen what poor little Nina's gone through, and while I'm not one of those idiots who think everyone should be alike even if it means mutilating them, I'd have to think twice if a kid of mine was born with wings. Hell, my daughter's got a tail, just a cute little one, and my wife and I had to give some pretty serious thought to whether she should keep it, let alone *wings*."

I had not ever before thought about it in those ways; I had just thought how fine and beautiful wings might be, and how glorious it would be to fly. I took a swig of beer and polished off my sandwich, then said, "But Nina's still got *her* wings."

"Sure does. Walt Parmenter insisted on keeping them. Partly he was just being a good father who didn't want to see her hurt, but he also thought it would be valuable to have a little girl who could fly, that it would be something people would pay to see, that she could do things ordinary people couldn't. And it got him killed."

I almost choked on my beer. "What?"

"About five, six years ago, some drifters, four of them, got drunk and decided they'd kidnap Nina and train her to steal for them, flying in upstairs windows or some damn fool thing like that, and Walt went after them, and it ended badly. We hanged the only drifter Walt left alive for us, but we weren't in time to keep Walt from bleeding to death."

"Nina wasn't hurt?"

"Oh, Nina was fine, except for hearing the whole fight—she didn't see it, they had her tied up in a sack. She had screaming nightmares for the next six months." He shook his head. "And she couldn't fly, anyway. They hadn't thought about that. If she *could*, then she would have just flown away home the minute they tried to make her work for their little scheme. They might not have been able to catch her in the first place, if she could fly."

"She really can't?"

"That's what she says, and it's what her mama says, and I figure they should know."

"It's a shame."

The bartender shrugged. "Walt wasn't a bad fellow, so that part's a shame, but I don't know Nina would be any better off if she could soar like a damn eagle."

I left it at that, but I thought to myself that having wings like that and not being able to *use* them was one of nature's nastier tricks.

When I'd finished my sandwich and beer I inquired whether there might be somewhere in town I could get a room, as I wasn't in any hurry to move on, and the bartender hesitated, frowning.

"Is there a problem?" I asked. "I'm not looking for trouble, I promise."

"Well, it's just..." He grimaced. "I do know someone with a room to let, but..."

He didn't seem inclined to finish the sentence, so I prompted him. "But what?"

"It's Dacey Parmenter. Nina's mother. I don't know that she'd want me referring you there after all your questions about little Nina."

"Ah," I said. "Mister, I respect what you're saying, but I'm not going to bother Nina. I get curious, yes, but I don't have any nefarious purpose here; I just need somewhere to sleep until I'm ready to move on again—or ready to find somewhere permanent, if I decide to settle here."

He still seemed a little reluctant, but he pointed. "Third house on the left on Front Street, the one with the fancy balconies. Don't tell her I sent you."

"Thanks," I said, leaving enough silver on the bar to cover my tab and a little more.

The house wasn't hard to find; I might have stumbled across it on my own, since the "Room to Let" sign in the window was plain to see. I went up on the porch and knocked.

I think I might have recognized Dacey Parmenter as Nina's mother even if I hadn't been told she was the landlady, as she resembled her daughter right to the dull brown hair.

No wings, though. She was a good bit taller, too, and wore her hair shorter than her daughter's.

I pointed to the sign in the window and said, "I could use a room."

She looked me over, and I tried to stand straight and look respectable. "For how long?" she asked.

"I don't know, ma'am. I'm traveling as the fancy takes me. I don't necessarily plan to stay in Damonsburg forever, but I'm not in a rush to move on, either."

She gave that a moment's thought, then shrugged. "I'll show you the room." She turned, and I followed her into the house.

Halfway up the stairs I remarked, "I believe I may have met your daughter."

I could see her shoulders tense. "Oh?"

"I suppose she might be some other kin, but she has your face. She and a couple of others were sitting on a fence by the Baker's Corner road. Seemed like nice kids. I'd never seen a girl with wings before."

She relaxed ever so slightly. "That's my Nina," she said. "You stay away from her."

"Didn't mean to worry you."

She didn't answer. We reached the top of the stairs and turned right, and she opened the door of the room. It was bright and airy with a big old canopy bed, the sheets and canopy white with bright red roses on them. A door on the far side opened onto one of those fancy balconies, overlooking the front lawn. I thought I'd enjoy sleeping in a room like that.

"What are you asking?" I said.

We settled on a price, meals included, and what currencies she would accept. I paid for a week, then set my pack down on the floor. She left, closing the door behind her, and I went out on the balcony.

Damonsburg looked even better from up there than it had from the street, full of flower gardens, and small shops, and rocking chairs on front porches—there were two on the Parmenter front porch, for that matter. I decided I'd definitely be staying for at least awhile.

I went back inside and unpacked, then went downstairs and out for a walk. I was thinking that if I intended to stay long I should probably find some honest work. I still had enough money hidden in my pack to live on for another year or two, but it wouldn't last forever, and I didn't like the idea that I wasn't earning my way in the world.

I hadn't found anything when suppertime rolled around, so I ambled back to the Parmenter house feeling a bit disappointed in myself. I went upstairs and dropped my hat on the bed, then went back downstairs and walked into the dining room as Nina was setting the table; I could hear her mother working in the kitchen.

"Hello," I said.

Nina looked up at me and frowned. "You're the new boarder?" she asked, in that sweet, soft voice of hers.

"That's right. Can I give you a hand?"

"No, I've got it, thank you." She went on setting out cutlery while I stood there, a little awkwardly, watching her while trying not to be obtrusive or rude.

She kept her wings folded down tight against her back, curving peaks thrust up above her head on either side, tips down by her ankles; even so, it seemed as if they were getting in the way whenever she had to reach to the side.

She finished, then stood by the kitchen door. A moment later her mother emerged holding a big pot of stew and spotted me.

"I wasn't sure you were going to make it, Mr. Smith," she said.

"And miss a proper home-cooked meal? I don't think so." I turned to Nina. "We still haven't been properly introduced."

Nina looked at me but didn't say anything.

Her mother frowned, and I remembered that she had told me to stay away from Nina, but then she relented. "Nina, this is Mr.

Smith. He's renting the front room. Mr. Smith, this is my daughter Nina; I understand you've met?"

I nodded. "This morning, on the road from Baker's Corner," I said. "It's a pleasure." I looked at the table and saw three place settings on a table big enough for at least six. "Just the three of us?"

Ms. Parmenter said, "You're the only boarder just now. If you'd take a seat, please?" She gestured toward one place—all three were at the far end of the table, mine on the right side. I sat there while the two of them made another trip to the kitchen and fetched out the rest of the meal.

"Would beer suit you, Mr. Smith?" Ms. Parmenter called, and I called back that it would suit me just fine.

Then they came back out and set everything on the table. Nina took the chair across from me, and Ms. Parmenter the one on the end.

We ate in awkward silence at first; neither of them spoke up, and as the guest it seemed as if it was my place to start the conversation, but I couldn't think of anything to talk about but Nina's wings—every time I looked up from my plate and started to open my mouth, there they were showing above her shoulders. I didn't think anything I might say about them would be welcome.

Then Ms. Parmenter took pity on me and said, "Where do you come from, Mr. Smith, and what brings you to Damonsburg?"

"Well, I grew up in Crooked Falls, down by the Blade Ruins," I said, and I went on to the whole story of what happened to my three sisters, and how my parents went away and left me with their wyrdstone, and how I sold it to my uncle and had to leave town when he decided I'd cheated him, which I had not.

"Been wandering ever since," I said. "I'm beginning to think about settling down for awhile, though."

"Here in Damonsburg?" Nina asked, and she didn't sound as if she was especially pleased with the idea.

I shrugged. "Maybe," I said. "Can't say I've seen anywhere better, as yet."

By that time we had polished off most of the stew, and Ms. Parmenter began clearing away. I offered to lend a hand, but she told me no.

"She doesn't like anyone else in her kitchen," Nina said. "Not even me."

"No?"

Nina grimaced. "No. I've knocked too many things off the shelves." She flexed her wings a little, to make her meaning clear.

I nodded. I didn't dare say anything; I hadn't yet learned what she might take offense at.

She stared at me a moment, then leaned across the table and whispered, "Was that story true?"

"What story?"

"About your family—your sisters, and your uncle."

I smiled. "Every word, I swear it."

"I wasn't sure. We've had some tale-spinners here."

"I'm not surprised. The worlds are full of them."

"But you aren't one of them?"

"Well, now, I won't say I haven't ever added a few arms or legs to a story to make it more interesting, but all in all I try to stick to the truth, and everything I told you tonight is just fact."

She smiled. "No extra arms or legs?"

"Not a one."

She nodded. "You said you've been traveling ever since you left your town?"

"Indeed I have."

"So where have you been? I saw you come up the road from Baker's Corner; what's it like there?"

So I told her about my stay in Baker's Corner, though that wasn't much of a tale. Ms. Parmenter cleared away the rest of the dinner leavings about then, and we got out of her way and went out on the front porch, where I told her about the Salt Coast, and Bootmaker Marsh, and Abbot's Creek, and half a dozen other places I'd visited.

I still had more to say when Ms. Parmenter came out on the porch and said, "Nina, time to come in and clean up."

"Yes, Momma." She hopped out of her rocking chair and went inside.

Ms. Parmenter paused and said "You two seem to have hit it off, Mr. Smith."

"Well, she's a good listener, ma'am, and like most men I love the sound of my own voice."

"She doesn't usually care for strangers. She's had some bad experiences."

I nodded. "I heard about what happened to her father."

"I asked you to stay away from her."

"You did. My apologies. I was just trying to be polite, answering her questions."

She stood for a moment, considering, then said, "She seems to like you."

I nodded. "I like her, certainly."

"Then you can talk to her, but only in this house. I don't want her following you around town."

"I'm fine with that, Ms. Parmenter."

She smiled, and followed her daughter into the house.

I sat a little longer, enjoying the cool of the evening and watching the firehawks draw lines of light in the sky over the distant mountains; then I went inside.

The next day I looked for work again, and this time I got an offer from the foreman at the sawmill east of town. It wasn't the best job I'd ever had, but it was steady work and paid well enough that I thought it would do until—well, unless—something better came along. I put in an honest afternoon's labor, then went home to the Parmenter house for supper.

It was roast chicken this time, rather than stew, and the conversation was easier—I told the Parmenters about my new job, and Nina told me about the feud in progress between two of her friends, Anna and Sybil.

"You met Sybil on your way into town," she said. "Anna was home sick."

"I hope it wasn't anything serious."

"Well, that's part of what they're fighting about." It seems that Anna was claiming she had been cursed by another girl they both disliked, and Sybil said that she would have cursed both of them so it must have been someone or something else, and...

I confess, I didn't follow all of it, but I enjoyed the sound of Nina's voice as she chattered away.

Again, we went out on the porch after we ate, just the two of us, and we talked. I told her more about my wanderings, and she told me more about her friends. Apparently she had about half a dozen close companions, while the rest of the children in town avoided her.

I decided to risk asking, "Do you think it's because of your wings?"

"Probably. And what my Daddy did when I was little."

I didn't answer at first, but at last I said, "I think I heard about that."

"He saved me from those men," she said, her face serious. "They deserved it."

"Why would it make anyone avoid you?"

"What he did to them. It was pretty horrible."

"I guess I didn't hear that part. All I heard was that he saved you from a bunch of drunken fools."

"He did, and they deserved it, but what people said..."

"Did you see what he did?"

She shook her head. "No. I was tied up in a big bag, and the people who found us didn't let me out until we were outside. They didn't want me to see. But people told me about it later. My Daddy cut them to pieces."

"Oh." I didn't say anything more for a moment, and neither did she, but at last I said, "He must have loved you very much."

"Uh huh." She sniffled a little.

"It's getting a bit chilly," I said.

She nodded.

"Should we go inside?"

She nodded again, and we did. I had thought we might continue our chat in the parlor, but she excused herself and headed up to her bedroom.

That was the pattern for the next week or so; I would work at the mill, come home and eat supper with the Parmenters, and then sit on the porch with Nina. Sometimes we talked, and sometimes we just sat and enjoyed each other's company. A couple of times one or two of her friends came by and joined the conversation; I was introduced, and each of them deemed me acceptable, indicating as much with a handshake. I got to re-tell some of my adventures, with Nina adding commentary along the way, warning our guests when a scary bit was coming, or telling them to get ready for some upcoming detail.

Ms. Parmenter remarked again on how well Nina and I got along. She said her girl didn't trust many adults.

"I don't blame her," I said. "Can't say that I trust many myself."

One evening, when it was just Nina and me on that front porch and no one else in sight, she started talking about her wings. She had opened them, as she sometimes did, to keep them from getting cramps, and had given them a firm shake that blew my hair in my eyes.

"Sometimes I wish I didn't have them," she said, as I brushed my hair back into place. "They get in the way, and grown-ups all treat me as if they're the only thing about me that matters."

"But they're so beautiful!" I said.

She shrugged, and her wings fluttered.

"Maybe if you could fly, you'd like them more."

"Maybe."

I hesitated, and then asked, "Why can't you fly?"

"Momma won't let me."

I sat silently for a moment, blinking in surprise. "That's it?" I asked. "You could fly if she said it was all right?"

"I don't know," Nina said. "Maybe."

"You haven't tried?"

"Momma said not to. I did try when I was little, but I kept running into things, and I hardly got off the ground, and once Daddy was gone Momma said I shouldn't do it any more, ever. So I haven't."

I nodded. "Your Momma probably knows what's best."

She looked up at the sky above the mountains. A lone firehawk went spiraling up from one of the peaks, and Nina said, "Sometimes I wonder what it would be like, though, seeing everything from above, and going wherever I wanted."

"I've gone wherever I pleased these last few years," I said. "There's something to be said for it, but I'm happy to stay here for a time."

She nodded, and folded her wings in.

It was about three days after that Dacey Parmenter met me on the porch as I came back from work.

"I think it might be time for you to move on, Mr. Smith," she said, as I came up the steps.

I stopped. "Oh? Why would that be, Ms. Parmenter?"

"Nina's spending too much time with you."

I considered that for a moment. "We enjoy each other's company, Ms. Parmenter. I don't mean her any harm."

"She's getting old enough that it's not safe for her to be hanging around older men."

"Ma'am, I never see her anywhere but in the house and on this porch."

"It's still too much."

"You could tell her not to come out to the porch with me."

"I could, yes, but I'd rather remove the temptation instead of giving her orders."

It seemed to me that she had already given Nina a pretty big order about not trying to fly, but maybe she was right. The more commandments she gave, the more Nina would be inclined to break a few. Fortunately, I thought I saw a way out of the situation that wouldn't force me to leave.

"If you like, I'll sit out on my balcony in the evenings, instead of the front porch," I suggested. "And when it gets too cold for that, I'll stay in my room instead of the parlor downstairs."

For a moment we stood silently face to face; then she said, "We can try that. I admit your rent money's welcome." She stepped aside to let me into the house, and called after me, "Dinner will be a little late."

We ate, and no mention was made of the new policy at the table. Afterward I went up to my room, rather than out to the porch, where I went out on the balcony and settled down with a book. I confess I missed Nina's company, but it was still a pleasant enough way to spend the evening. I finished the book and went to bed.

The following day I stopped at an antique shop on my way home and bought another book, as I had exhausted my personal library. I read about half of it that night.

On the third day of the new regime Nina asked me at the table, "Why don't you sit out on the porch anymore?"

Ms. Parmenter tensed.

"I wanted a change of pace," I said.

"I miss talking to you."

"You could visit one of your friends, couldn't you?"

"No! I'm not allowed in their houses; I knock things over." She spread her wings slightly, then folded them back down, to make clear what she meant. "We always play outside, but most of them aren't allowed outside after dark."

"You could invite them over here."

She glanced at her mother. "Maybe," she said.

We finished eating; I excused myself and headed upstairs. I could feel Nina's gaze following me.

I had been on the balcony, reading, for perhaps half an hour when I heard Nina's voice. I took my feet off the rail, closed my book, leaned over, and looked down at the front lawn.

Nina was standing there, looking up at me.

"Did I do something wrong?" she called.

I held a finger to my lips, then shook my head.

Nina looked toward the front door, then up at me. She hesitated.

Then she spread her wings, and flapped.

She was a bit awkward at first, but by the time she was high enough to grab the railing of my balcony she seemed to have it under control. She hung there on the outside of the railing, slipped her feet between the uprights, folded her wings, and demanded, "Why aren't you talking to me anymore?"

"You flew up here!" I said, astonished. "I thought you couldn't fly!"

She ignored my words. "Why aren't you *talking* to me?"

She was clearly not going to be satisfied with any sort of evasion, and I did not want to lie to her. "Your mother asked me not to," I said. "She thinks a girl your age shouldn't be spending so much time with a man my age."

"My age? I'll be twelve next month!"

"That's the point. I think she's worried you might have a crush on me, and that I might take advantage of that."

She stared at me for a moment, then said, "Oh."

"She's your mother. She wants to protect you."

Nina frowned. "But... she doesn't need to protect me from *you*."

"Well, *I* don't think so, and *you* don't think so, but she doesn't *know* whether she can trust me. Or you, for that matter. She told you not to try to fly, and here you are."

"She doesn't know..."

"Have you been flying when she wasn't around?"

"No! This is the first time, I swear it!"

I believed her.

"I *did* fly, didn't I?"

"You really did."

Just then we heard the front door slam, and Ms. Parmenter calling, "Nina! Are you out here?"

"Oh!" Nina said, spreading her wings.

And then she flew away, up and over the top of the house, as her mother came down the steps calling for her.

Ms. Parmenter looked up—she probably heard the sound of her wings—but not in time to see her before she was out of sight over the edge of the roof.

"Mr. Smith," she called, "have you seen Nina?"

"Is she missing?"

"I don't know where she went!"

"I'm sure she's fine."

Ms. Parmenter looked up and down the street, obviously worried, then turned and went back into the house.

I decided I had better reassure her. I put my book away and headed down the stairs, and found Ms. Parmenter in the front hall, and Nina emerging from the kitchen. She must have come in the back door.

"There you are!" Ms. Parmenter exclaimed.

"Here I am," Nina said.

I stood at the foot of the stairs and watched as Ms. Parmenter hurried toward her daughter.

Nina took a step back, though, and spread her wings as far as she could inside the house.

"Momma," she said, "I can fly."

Ms. Parmenter stopped dead in her tracks.

"It's wonderful," Nina said. "I'm not going to stop."

Ms. Parmenter stared at her for a long silent moment, her face frozen. Then she nodded.

"Just be careful," she said, and her voice shook. Without another word she turned aside.

I stayed through the winter. Nina and I spoke on the porch sometimes, but sometimes she was flying, exploring her world's new possibilities, and I would sit and read. I would look up occasionally to see the firehawks over the mountains, and the red and gold of Nina's wings catching their light. When the snows came I watched Nina dance among the snowflakes as they fell, and saw her land with her wings speckled with white and her face alight with joy. We spoke less and less often, as she used her new freedom to find new places and new people.

And in the spring I decided I had had enough of Damonsburg and headed out, my pack on my shoulder. Nina gave me a hug before I left, and she flew along overheard for a mile or so, looking down at me, before she turned to go home.

When Hell Froze Over

At the time we all thought it was a really clever idea, one of the best that the boss had ever come up with. It was one of those things that nobody ever thinks of, until someone does, and then it's just so *obvious* that you sit there saying, "Why didn't *I* think of that?"

And really, it was great fun at the time, despite how it all turned out.

It seemed like such a simple thing. For centuries, people had been promising to do this, that, or the other when Hell froze over—so the boss thought, why *not* freeze it over?

I mean, sure, burning's about the most painful thing possible, and we had an obligation to keep all those damned souls suffering, but after ten thousand years you can get used to *anything*, and the older souls were taking it all in stride, getting really complacent about it—"Ho, hum, another flame; how hot is *this* one? Sulphur and napalm—didn't we do that *last* week? White phosphorus was good—when do you think we'll have that again?"

Satan hates it when his people get complacent.

Besides, he's always liked to shake things up—that's how he wound up running Hell in the first place, isn't it? He got thinking about expectations and surprises, and just how nasty a good cold spell can be, and how sometimes something's worse if you get a break from it for awhile. And there were all those thousands and thousands of promises.

So he started planning it all out, in private.

Well, of course, in private; he wanted it to be a surprise. Wouldn't do to have people expecting it, as if it were a vacation or something. Pleased anticipation is *not* something the damned are entitled to.

Besides, the technical aspects were tricky. The heat isn't just something we *do*, after all, it's the natural climate down here. And changing that, all at once, everywhere, dropping the temperature a couple of hundred degrees for a week—he figured a week would be about right—and then bringing it back up to normal again, that was quite a challenge.

Sure, the boss has what you might call supernatural talents, but he's not *God*, after all—that's why he's *down* here, instead of running the universe. And he put most of what power he had into seeing that all those old promises were kept—after all, people wouldn't even *know* that Hell had frozen over without a little help.

To this day, I don't know all the details of how he did it. I know the basic technique, which was pretty hard to ignore, but I suppose...

Oh, you don't know how it was done? Basically, the tech crew just blew the entire atmosphere of Hell—everything, air, brimstone, all of it—out into hard vacuum somewhere in interstellar space, to dump most of the heat. That added a nice little twist, as it left everybody strangling for a few hours, until the ice arrived.

I think the ice came from a cometary cloud somewhere— must've been enough raw mass for half a dozen fair-sized planets, all hitting the ground at once. *Hot* ground—the old atmosphere didn't carry off *all* the heat, and vacuum's a good insulator, the best.

So all the slush and ice in the first wave flashed up into steam on impact, and we had air again, after a fashion—and then the next wave hit, and the next, and we had people crushed and splattered all over. If they hadn't already been dead, we'd probably have lost the entire population, one way or another.

I'll tell you, there wasn't *anybody* out there thinking this was a winter vacation! None of them—none of *us*, because we lower-level types hadn't been told yet—had the faintest idea what in Hell was going on. We thought maybe it was Armageddon, and they'd changed the rules on us somehow.

Anyway, after the first three batches of ice, Hell was down below room temperature, with slush and ice water everywhere, and damp fog that was nearly as hard to breathe or see through as the smoke had been.

But it wasn't frozen over—just cold and clammy.

And then, after a day or so, when we were getting used to it, when we had just about everybody dug out—well, I don't know how they did it, but that was when the *real* cold hit. Went down to about eighty below in maybe an hour and a half.

The air was clear and sharp, like nothing I'd ever seen, and it seemed to cut right into you when the wind blew. All that wet ground froze hard as iron, with sheet ice everywhere—all those meltwater pools were slick and smooth as a con-man's pitch, and a lot of the damned were frozen into the ice.

And that was when they broke out the skates. Millions of them. You see, for some people, the saying was, "When they ice skate in Hell."

Or ski; I didn't get skis, but some demons did.

And it was when they brought around the equipment that they finally told us what was going on, and we all admired the idea. We wanted to do our part, so we got out there and we skated and skied, gliding over the ice, and over the frozen souls when we found them handy.

But you know, we hadn't thought it through. All that time, when we were down there skating and skiing and watching those poor damned folks wishing they could freeze to death and get it over with, we were figuring that it meant more business, that we'd be getting more customers as a result.

We were all wrong.

Sure, it's obvious *now*, but it caught us by surprise. We all knew people made promises they said they'd keep when Hell froze over, but we hadn't thought about what *kind* of promises, what sort of prophecies we were fulfilling.

"You won't get your money back until Hell freezes over!"

"They'll ice-skate in Hell before this is fixed!"

"Forgive you? It'll be a cold day in Hell!"

So the boss had delivered a cold day in Hell—and when we saw the reports later, we were flat-out amazed by the wave of forgiveness, of fairness and justice and people doing things they should have done long ago.

Cut our incoming business in half for a good six months.

Old Satan caught on fast enough, and cut the whole thing short, so we only got three days instead of a week, but the damage had been done. Took almost a month to get the fires going again and boil off all that water, and I don't think we've got everything up to its proper temperature even yet.

That about did it for experimentation for the next few millennia. Unless...

Well, while we were out there skating over all that ice, a few of us got talking, and we came up with this idea we've sent up through channels. It's been working its way up through the chain of command for a couple of years now. I don't suppose it'll go over, really, after the way the ice turned out, but I think it could really be great. It'd be right there on Earth, not down here, so it wouldn't disrupt everything here—but it would drive all those rationalists up there buggy. Might do some serious damage to common sense, which is one of our worst enemies when it comes to recruiting. Sure, we'd have a few promises we'd rather not see kept, but nowhere near as many of them, and I, for one, think it'd be worth it.

Ever heard the phrase, "When pigs fly?"

About the Author:

Lawrence Watt-Evans has been a full-time writer for more than forty years, with more than fifty novels and well over a hundred short stories to his credit, as well as assorted essays, poems, comic books, and so on. His story "Why I Left Harry's All-Night Hamburgers" won the 1988 Hugo for short story, as well as the Asimov's Readers Award. He lives in Bainbridge Island, Washington with his wife.

His website is at www.watt-evans.com.

www.ingramcontent.com/pod-product-compliance
Lightning Source LLC
Chambersburg PA
CBHW051437170626
46809CB00006B/2506